WINNETOU

THE TREASURE OF NUGGET MOUNTAIN

Karl May

Translated and adapted by Marion Ames Taggart
from the original German

Printed on acid free paper in the USA

British Library Cataloguing In Publication Data
A Record of this Publication is available
from the British Library

ISBN 978-1-84685-801-7

This edition first published 2007 by
Diggory Press

Diggory Press Ltd
Three Rivers, Minions, Liskeard, Cornwall, PL14 5LE, UK
Diggory Press, Inc.,
Goodyear, Arizona, 85338, USA
WWW.DIGGORYPRESS.COM

**Publish <u>your</u> book internationally with Diggory Press!
See our website for details**

WINNETOU

THE TREASURE OF NUGGET MOUNTAIN

CHAPTER I

A JOURNEY AND A MEETING

IT is certainly true that no man knows what the future holds for him. When I, Jack Hildreth, newly graduated from college, won the consent of my uncle and second father, whose namesake and heir I was, to go West to see life, I little dreamed of the experience that lay before me. I had gone as a civil engineer to survey for a railroad that was to run through the lands of the Apaches, in the mountains of Arizona and New Mexico. The greatest chief of all the Apache tribes was Intschu-Tschuna, and he and his son Winnetou had defeated the attempted unjust invasion of their rights, had slain all my comrades, except the three scouts who accompanied us, and it was only by showing that courage and skill which the red man so profoundly admires that I succeeded in convincing the Indians that I was trustworthy, and saving myself and the scouts, Sam Hawkins, Dick Stone, and Will Parker, from death by torture. But once having accepted me, there was no reservation in their love for me. I had been made a full son of Intschu-Tschuna, and a brother of Winnetou by drinking the blood of that true knight of the plains, as he had drunk mine, and our kinship and brotherhood was not one in name merely, but in very truth and deed, for I had come to love and admire the high-minded, brave young Indian as I have never before or since loved another friend, and his love for me was equally strong.

A whole winter had passed since the morning in late autumn when the Apaches burst upon us and put an end to the work on which we were sent. It had been a winter of the greatest interest, passed as it was in closest intimacy with Intschu-Tschuna, Winnetou, and his beautiful young sister Nscho-Tschi, the Fair Day, who, when I first came among the Apaches, and was still under sentence of death as a traitor and a thief of their lands, had been my gentle nurse through a long and dangerous fever.

Winnetou had not only taught me the Apache tongue, but also all that skill in hunt and warfare which has been the Indian's inheritance for countless generations, and of which he was a master. Intschu-Tschuna made me wise in the lore of his people, and the sweet Fair Day showed me that a loving daughter and sister, a true-hearted and gentle maiden, was to the red Indian, as to the white, his most precious possession.

But the pleasantest life must end, the sunniest days pass. When the spring came I told Intschu-Tschuna that I must go back to my home in the distant East, though I would return later to my new and faithful friends. The chief's face grew sad at these tidings, but he said: "Intschu-Tschuna feared that his white son would go to the sea in the rising sun, even as the rivers flow toward it when the winter is past. Will you stay with those pale-faces who would have built the railroad?"

"No."

"That is right. You have become a brother of the red man, and ought not have any share in further attempts on his lands and property. But where you wish to go you cannot live by the chase as you can here. Winnetou has told me that you would have had money had we not come upon you and stopped your work, and he has asked me to make this up to you. The red men know the places where gold is found; they need only take it away. Do you wish me to get some for you?"

Others in my place might have said yes eagerly, and received nothing, but I saw the peculiar keenness of his eyes as they watched me, and answered, "I thank you. There is no satisfaction in riches that a man gets without effort; only that for which he has labored and struggled possesses value."

His gaze softened; he gave me his hand, and said heartily: "Your words tell me that we are not deceived in you. The golden dust for which the white gold hunters strive is a deadly dust. It destroys those who find it. Never seek it, for it kills not only the body but the soul. I wanted to try you. I would not have given you gold, but you shall receive money, the very money on which you counted."

"That is not possible."

"It is possible, for I will it so. We will go back to where you were working. You shall continue your work, and thus receive the reward promised you for doing it."

I looked at him amazed and speechless. Could he be jesting? No; such a thing would be impossible to the dignity of an Indian chief. Or was it another test?

"My young white brother says nothing," continued the chief." Is my offer not acceptable to him?"

"On the contrary, more acceptable than I can say, but I cannot believe that you are in earnest."

"Why not?"

"Am I to understand that I am to complete the work for which my white comrades were punished with death? That I am to do that for which you rebuked me so sternly when we first met?"

"You acted then without the permission of the owners of the land, but now you shall receive this permission. The offer is not mine, but Winnetou's. He says it will not harm us if you complete the interrupted work."

"That is a mistake. The road will be built; the white men will certainly come."

He looked gloomily before him, and after a short pause said: "You are right. We cannot prevent our selves being robbed again and yet again. First they send a little band, such as yours was, which we could overcome. But that counts as nothing, for later they will come in crowds, before which we must retreat, or be destroyed. But neither can you alter this. Or do you mean that they will not come if you do not finish your measuring?"

"No, I do not mean that, for do what we will, the fire steed will come through all this region."

"Then accept my offer. It will help you, and can do us no harm. I have talked with Winnetou. We will ride with you, he and I, and thirty braves, which will be enough to protect your labor, and can help you. Then we will take these braves as far East as is necessary to find safe paths, and we will go by the steam canoe to St. Louis."

"What is my red brother saying? Do I understand him aright? He will go East?"

"Yes; I and Winnetou, and Nscho-Tschi."

"Nscho-Tschi also?"

"My daughter also. She would be glad to see the great dwelling places of the pale-faces, and stay among them till she has become like a white squaw."

I must have looked amazed at this news, for the chief added smilingly: "My young white brother seems to be astonished. If he has any objection to our accompanying him let him say so frankly."

"Any objection! How could I have any? On the contrary it delights me. Under your protection I should be safe, and that alone would be a great deal, but, above all, I should still have with me those who are so dear to me."

"How," he assented, quite satisfied." then you shall finish your work, and we will go Eastward. Can Nscho-Tschi find people with whom she can live, and who will teach her?"

"Yes; I will gladly make that my care. She shall go to a house where there are none but good ladies who pray to the Great Spirit, and teach the young maidens of the pale-faces."

"Good. And when will my young white brother be ready?"

"Whenever it pleases you."

"Then we will go at once. Winnetou has already arranged for this, and my young white son need feel no care."

We were to start in two days, yet the peaceful life in the pueblo was not disturbed; even Nscho-Tschi served us at meal-time as calmly as usual. What a fuss her white sisters make over a small excursion, yet this Indian girl, with a long, dangerous ride before her, and all the customs of civilization to learn, showed no trace of excitement in her manner.

At last came the morning of the departure. We made short work of breakfast, for the ceremony of consulting the medicine-man as to the success of the journey was to be performed. All the men, women and children of the pueblo came out to take part in this ceremony, which was not unlike the Greeks consulting the oracle, or the Romans reading the auguries. A sort of sanctuary hung with blankets was prepared for the medicine-man, and behind this he retired, and a circle of Apaches formed around him. Then he began a kind of growling and snarling, like dogs and cats beginning a fight, the growling occasionally broken by a howl, which sank into softer tones. The howl meant that the medicine-man had seen something bad in the future; the softer notes announced something good. After this had continued some time, the medicine-man burst forth from his improvised temple, and ran round the circle shrieking like a madman. This performance was followed by a dance, slow and grotesque, made more so by the fact that he wore a horrible mask, and had all sorts of curious and ugly objects hung over his body, and the dance was accompanied by an intoned song. Both song and dance were violent at first, becoming quieter by degrees, till at last the medicine-man seated himself, his head between his knees, and remained silent and motionless for a long time. At last he sprang up, and announced the result of his inquiry.

"Hear, hear, ye sons and daughters of the Apaches! This is what Manitou, the great good Spirit has revealed to me. Intschu-Tschuna and Winnetou the Apache chiefs, and Old Shatterhand, who has become our white chief, will ride to the dwelling place of the pale-faces. The good Manitou will protect them. They will go through many adventures without harm, and will come back to us safely. Nscho-Tschi too, who will stay longer among the palefaces, will come back to us safely, and there is but one of them whom we shall never see again."

He paused, and his head was bowed as if to show his grief over this last announcement.

"Ugh, ugh, ugh," cried the Indians, curious to hear more, yet not daring to ask. But as the medicine-man remained bowed down and silent, little Sam Hawkins, my true friend and faithful comrade, lost patience and cried: "Who is it that will not return? Let the man of medicine tell us."

For a long time there was no reply; then the medicine man raised his head slowly, looked at me, and said: "It were better not to have asked. But since Sam Hawkins, the curious pale-face, has forced me to say it, I will tell you it is Old Shatterhand who will never return. Death will seize him in a short time. They who would come back safely must not stay near him, for they who are near him shall be in danger, and they who are at a distance from him shall be safe. How!"

Now Old Shatterhand was the name that had been given to me, because of the reputation my strong hands had earned in knocking down any one who attacked me. Intschu-Tschuna and Winnetou glanced at each other as they heard these words. One could not say whether or not they believed them, but they knew the fatal effect of the words on those men whom they had picked out to protect us. If they believed it dangerous to be near me the safety of the entire party would be imperiled. Intschu-Tschuna took both my hands, and speaking very loud so that every one could hear, reminded his people that the medicine-man had sometimes made mistakes in his prophecies, and that only time could show whether he had spoken truly in this instance. Scarcely were his last words uttered than Sam Hawkins stepped forth and said: "No, we need not leave it to time. There is a means by which we can discover at once whether the medicine-man has announced the truth. Not only the red men, but the white have their medicine-men who can read the future, and I, Sam Hawkins, am the most renowned among them."

"Ugh, ugh," cried the Apaches amazed.

"Yes, you wonder at that. Heretofore you have considered me an ordinary trapper, because you did not know me. But you shall find out that I know more than my prayers. Let some of my red brothers dig a small, but deep hole in the earth with their tomahawks."

"Would my white brother look into the middle of the earth?" asked Intschu-Tschuna.

"Yes; for the future lies hidden in the bosom of the earth and in the stars, and since I cannot read the stars in broad daylight, I must turn to the earth for that which I wish to know."

Some of the Indians had at once complied with his request, and were digging a hole with their tomahawks.

"Don't try any humbug, Sam," I whispered. "If the Indians see through your nonsense it will make matters worse."

"Humbug! Nonsense!" he retorted. "What are the medicine-man's practices but humbug and nonsense? What he can and dare do, I can and dare do also, my cautious young professor. I know what I'm about. If nothing is done to reassure them we shan't be able to do anything with the men who go with us."

"I know that, but I beg you not to do anything ridiculous."

"Oh, it's solemn, perfectly solemn; don't you worry."

In spite of his assurance I felt considerable anxiety; I knew him too well. He was a born joker, and forever up to some trick, but I had no chance to say more, for he walked away to tell the Indians how deep to make the hole. When everything was ready, Sam took off his old leather hunting jacket, rolled it up, and set it over the hole like a cylinder, where the stiff old coat stood up as if made of wood.

"Now," said Sam to his audience, "the men, women, and children of the Apaches shall see what I do, and wonder at it. When I have spoken my magic words the earth shall open her bosom to me, and I will see what is to happen to us during our journey." with this he went back a few paces, approached the hole with slow and solemn steps, to my horror repeating the multiplication table from the ones up to the nines, but he did so too rapidly for the Indians to catch what he said. When he got to the end of the table of nines, he broke into a gallop, sprang up to the coat with a loud howl, waving his arms like a windmill. I looked around to see what the Indians thought of this performance, and to my great relief saw that they all looked perfectly serious; even the two chiefs betrayed no doubt in their faces, though I was sure that Intschu-Tschuna knew right well what Sam was up to.

Sam kept his head down in the coat a good five minutes, moving his arms the while as if he saw marvelous things. At last he raised his head, showing a face solemn to the last degree, shook out his coat, and drew it on again, saying: "My red brothers may fill in the hole again. While it is open I can say nothing." this was done, and Sam drew a deep breath, as if he felt deeply impressed, and said: "Our red brother has seen wrong, for exactly the contrary of what he said is to happen. I have seen all that is to come to pass in the coming week, but it is forbidden me to repeat it all. I have heard shots, and seen a struggle. The last shot came from Old Shatterhand's bear-killer, and he who fires the last shot cannot have died, but must be the victor. My red brothers can be safe only by keeping close to Old Shatterhand. If they obey their medicine-man they are lost. I have spoken. How!"

The consequences of this prophecy were exactly what Sam had anticipated, at least for the time. The Indians evidently believed him, and as the medicine-man did not come forth to oppose Sam's statement he was considered vanquished, and Sam the true prophet. Winnetou's eyes rested on Sam, who had come chuckling over to me, with a silent, but very expressive look, while his father said: "My white brother is a wise man; he has taken the force from the words of our medicine-man, and he has a coat full of wise sayings. This precious coat will be honored from one big water to the other. But Sam Hawkins should not have gone so far. It was enough to say that Old Shatterhand would bring us no evil; why did he prophesy anything bad?"

"Because I saw it in the hole."

Intschu-Tschuna made a gesture dismissing this statement, and said: "Intschu-Tschuna knows the truth; Sam Hawkins can be sure of that. It was not necessary to make our people anxious by speaking of bad things to come. Let us go."

The horses were brought, and we mounted, and rode slowly away from the pueblo village, Intschu-Tschuna, Winnetou, his sister and I ahead, Sam Hawkins, Parker and Stone following, and behind them the thirty braves leading the pack horses. Nscho-Tschi sat astride her horse like a man. She was a remarkably daring and accomplished rider, as I knew already, and as she proved anew on this journey, and she could handle weapons equally well. Any one meeting us would have taken her for the younger brother of Winnetou, the likeness between them being heightened by her masculine garments; but they only brought out more clearly her remarkable beauty. She was so radiant, so happy, so girlish, in spite of the knife and pistol in her belt, and the gun across her shoulders that all eyes turned on her admiringly. Poor, beautiful Fair Day!

After five days we reached the spot where we had been working when taken prisoners by the Apaches, and the rest of the party was cut down in the struggle. Here I resumed my work, guarded by the Apache braves, and helped by Winnetou and Nscho-Tschi, who scarcely left my side. It was very different from the circumstances under which I had labored before, with a band of drinking, unprincipled adventurers for companions. Now I was with friends, and I was profoundly touched by the generous proof of affection they gave me in allowing me to finish a work begun in dishonesty to them, now that they were convinced that I had no part in the wrong intended them, and that the completion of the work would be to my advantage. No brother could have been more lovingly watchful of my welfare than my brother, the Apache, and his father helped me in every way in his power, but it was Nscho-Tschi who anticipated my every wish, seeming to read my thoughts, and no desire of mine was too trivial for her to take infinite pains to gratify. Every day increased the grateful affection I felt for her, which I could only show by teaching her all that she was so eager to learn. Dear, bright, devoted little sister! Sweet Fair Day, so soon to set!

At the end of the eighth day I had finished; the instruments were repacked, and we resumed our journey Eastward over the same route I had traveled in coming West under the guidance of Sam Hawkins. It was the second day after we had set out on our long ride that we saw four white men coming toward us. They were dressed like cowboys, armed with guns, knives and revolvers. When they had come within twenty feet of us they reined up, took their guns in their hands as a precautionary measure, and called to us: "Good day, gentlemen. Must we keep our fingers on our triggers or not?"

"Good day," replied Sam. "Put up your shooting irons; we've no desire to eat you. May we ask where you came from?"

"From old father Mississippi."

"We're going the way you came; is it open?"

"Yes, as far as we know, but any way you needn't fear with a party of your size. Or aren't the red men going all the way?"

"Only this warrior here, with his daughter and son; they are Intschu-Tschuna and Winnetou, the Apache chiefs."

"You don't say so! A red belle going to St. Louis? May we ask your names?"

"Why not? We're not ashamed of them. These are my comrades Dick Stone and Will Parker, and this is Old Shatterhand, a boy who has stabbed the grizzly with his knife, and knocks down the strongest men with his fist. I am Sam Hawkins. And you?"

"I am called Santer," said the leader, and after a few more questions they rode on.

Then Winnetou said to Sam: "Why has my brother told these strangers so much about us? I do not trust the politeness of that pale-face. He was polite only because we were eight times as many as they. I am not pleased that you should have told them who we were."

"Why? Do you think it can do any harm?"

"Yes."

"In what way?"

"In many ways. The man who spoke to you has bad eyes; I must know what he does. My brothers may go slowly forward, and I will go back with Old Shatterhand to follow these pale-faces, and see whether they really went on, or only pretended to do so."

Accordingly Winnetou and I turned back upon our way, and followed the strangers. I confess the man Santer had struck me exactly as he had Winnetou.

10

"Does my brother see," said the young chief when we were out of hearing of the others, "that if these men were thieves they would know we had gold with us? Sam Hawkins was so imprudent as to say we were chiefs on our way to St. Louis, and they need know no more. For such a journey gold is necessary, yet if they attacked us today they would find none, but tomorrow we shall get all that we require, and there was no use in bringing more than we could use. To-morrow we will go to the place where it is hidden, and bring away enough for our journey."

"Is the place where you get gold on our way?"

"Yes, it is in a mountain called Nugget-tsil, or Gold Mountain, though it has another name in the mouths of those who do not know that gold is there."

I was amazed to hear this. Think of these men knowing where gold was hidden in such quantities, and yet living a life of such hardship and danger!

By this time we had followed Santer far enough on his course to feel sure that he had no intention of turning back. We reined up, and watched their retreating figures till they looked like flies on the horizon, then turned our horses to rejoin our party.

"Come," said Winnetou, "they intend no evil, and we can rest secure."

Neither he nor I guessed with what a cunning wretch we had to deal, who realizing he would be watched, had ridden so far to throw us off our guard.

We returned to our camp, and the chief, and Nscho-Tschi, feeling perfectly secure, little dreaming that the strangers in turn were following us, with death in their hearts and hands.

CHAPTER II

TO NUGGET MOUNTAIN

THAT night we encamped beside a spring, which flowed fresh and bright from the tender grass it watered, and was most acceptable to our tired horses. The spot was surrounded by bushes and trees which enabled us to have a fire without its being seen at a great distance. Two sentinels were stationed by the chief to watch, and everything seemed to insure our safety as we sat around the fire, sheltered from the cool night wind by the bushes.

It was our custom in the pueblo to sit and talk after supper, and we did so to-night. In the course of the conversation Intschu-Tschuna said that we should not resume our journey in the morning until mid-day, and when Sam Hawkins asked why this was he was answered with a frankness which I profoundly regretted later: "That should be a secret, but I can trust it to my white brothers, if they will promise not to try to know more than I tell them."

We all gave the promise, and he continued: "We need gold, so tomorrow morning early I will go with my children to get nuggets, and shall return at midday."

Stone and Parker uttered an exclamation of wonder, and Sam, no less amazed, asked: "Is there gold near here?"

"Yes," replied Intschu-Tschuna. "No one suspects it; even my braves do not know it. I learned it from my father, who in turn had the secret from his father. Such secrets are always handed down from father to son, and considered sacred; they are not shared even with one's dearest friends. It is true I have now spoken of it, but I would not tell any man the place, nor show it to him, and I would shoot down any one who dared follow us to discover it."

"Would you kill even us?"

"Even you. I have trusted you, and if you betrayed that trust you would deserve to die. But I know you will not leave this spot till we have returned."

With this he ended the subject abruptly, and the conversation took another turn. Intschu-Tschuna, Winnetou, Nscho-Tschi and I sat with our backs toward the bushes; Sam, Dick and Will on the opposite side of the fire facing us. In the midst of our pleasant talk Hawkins suddenly uttered a cry, snatched his gun, and fired between us into the thicket. Of course his shot alarmed the entire camp. The Indians rushed over to us, and we jumped up, demanding of Sam why he had fired.

"I saw two eyes shining out of the bushes behind Intschu-Tschuna," he declared. Instantly the Indians snatched brands from the fire, and rushed into the shrubbery. Their search was vain. We quieted down at last, and seated ourselves as before. "Sam Hawkins must have been mistaken," said Intschu-Tschuna. "Such mistakes are easily made in the flickering fire's light."

"I don't see how I could be," said Sam. "I felt perfectly sure I saw two eyes there."

"The wind turned the leaves; my brother saw the light side, and took them for eyes."

"That's possible, and in that case I must have killed the leaves."

He laughed in his silent way, but Winnetou did not look at the matter in the light of a jest; he said gravely: "In any case my brother Sam has made a great mistake, for which we may pay later."

"A mistake? How so?"

"The shot was dangerous for us," said Winnetou.. "Either Sam saw no eyes, and then it was unnecessary, and would attract our enemies who might be about, or, if he really saw a man, the shot was foolish, for it could not hit him possibly."

"Oh, but Sam Hawkins is sure of his aim; I don't miss my mark."

"I too can shoot, but in such a case I certainly should not have hit. The spy would have seen you take your gun, and would move out of your range."

Though the others were satisfied with the search that had been made Winnetou did not accept it as final. Once more he rose, and went out to go over the ground again himself, and make sure all was well. He was gone over an hour, and when he came back he said: "There is no man there; Sam Hawkins must certainly have been mistaken."

Nevertheless he doubled the sentinels, bidding them be more than usually vigilant, and patrol the circle of our camp more frequently. Then we lay down to rest. My sleep was not quiet; I waked often, and during my naps had brief, turbulent dreams in which Santer and his comrades played the chief parts. That was the natural consequence of our meeting him, and the alarm of the evening, but I could not shake off the impression of dread these dreams left.

After a breakfast of dried meat, and a porridge of meal and water, Intschu-Tschuna with his son and daughter started away. Before they went I implored them to let me accompany them, at least part of the way, and lest they should suspect me of wanting to discover the hiding-place of the gold, I told them that I could not get rid of the thought of Santer. I wondered at myself, for unlikely as it was, I felt that he had come back. "My brother need not be anxious for us," answered Winnetou. "In order to satisfy him I will look again at the trail. We know that he does not think of the gold, but if he came with us part of the way he would suspect where it lay, and he would catch the fever for the deadly dust that never leaves a pale-face till soul and body are destroyed. We beg him not to go with us, not because we distrust him, but because of our love and foresight."

After this I had to be silent. Winnetou looked again for a trace of other feet than ours, discovered nothing, and they went away. They were not mounted, so I knew the spot where they were going could not be far.

I lay down in the grass and smoked, and tried to talk with my comrades, but I could not rest. At last I sprang up, took my gun, and wandered forth, thinking I might find some game which would serve for our dinner, and help divert my thoughts. Intschu-Tschuna had gone southward from the camp, so I went northward, that he might not think I was searching for the forbidden path. After I had walked a quarter of an hour I came, to my surprise, on a trail, the fresh footprints of three persons. They wore moccasins, and I distinguished two large, two medium sized, and two little feet. It must be Intschu-Tschuna, Winnetou, and Nscho-Tschi. They had gone southward to mislead us, and had then gone due north. Dared I go further? No. It was possible that they saw me, it was certain that on their return they would discover my footprints, and might think I had followed them secretly. Still I could not go back to camp, so I wandered easterly a short distance further.

Suddenly I stopped short, for I had come upon another trail. Examination showed it to be the footprints of men with spurs, and I instantly thought of Santer. The trail ran in the direction where the two chiefs must be, and seemed to come from some shrubbery a little further on. I went there. I was right; the trail did come from these bushes, and there I found tied the four horses which had been ridden by Santer and his companions the day before. Evidently the wretches had hidden here all night, and Sam Hawkins had not been mistaken, but had really seen a pair of eyes. We had been spied upon, and -- Ah, heavens! What a thought came to me now! What had we been talking of just before Sam fired? Of Intschu-Tschuna and his children going today to get the gold. This had been heard, and now, the rascals were following my friends. Winnetou in danger! And Nscho-Tschi and her father! Instantly I mounted, and rode for life and death on the trail. There was no time to go back and alarm the camp; if only I could be in time! I tried to guess where the hiding-place of the gold might be, in case I lost the trail. Winnetou had spoken of a mountain called Nugget-tsil, or Nugget Mountain, so the place was a hill. I looked over the scene through which I was flying and north of me, directly in my path, saw a considerable elevation crowned by woods.

This then must be Nugget Mountain. The old nag under me was not swift enough, so as I passed I pulled a branch from a bush and belabored him with it. He did his best, and the plain disappeared behind me; the hills rose before my eyes. The trail led between two of them, and was lost in the stones which covered their sides, but I did not dismount, for I knew those I sought had gone farther into the valley. At last I was forced to get down, and try to discover the trail. It was not easy to do, but at last I succeeded; it led into the ravine. The horse could only hinder me here, so I tied him to a tree, and hurried on afoot, impelled by fear to a haste that took away my breath. I had to pause a moment for breath on a cliff, and saw the trail plunge to the left into the woods. I ran under the trees which grew farther apart as I advanced, and spied an opening ahead of me. I had not quite reached it when I heard several shots. In an instant a cry arose that pierced my very flesh like a sword. It was the death cry of the Apaches. I not only ran, I sprang forward in long leaps like a wild beast.

Again a shot, then another. That was Winnetou's rifle. Thank God, then he was not dead. I had but one more spring to make to be in the clearing, but for an instant I stood petrified by what I saw. The light was dim, but directly before me lay Intschu-Tschuna and his daughter; I could not tell whether they were alive or dead. A little way beyond was a small crag behind which stood Winnetou reloading his rifle. To my left, protected by trees, were two men with guns aimed at Winnetou, while a third crept cautiously under the trees to get behind him. The fourth lay at my feet, shot through the head.

For the moment the young chief was in greater danger from the two, than the third. I took my bear-killer and shot them both down. Then without taking time to re-load I sprang behind the third man. He saw me coming, and aimed at me. I leaped aside; the shot did not touch me. He saw his game was up, and ran into the woods. I rushed after him, for it was Santer, and I wanted to capture him. But the distance between us was too great; he disappeared in the darkness of the thick forest, and I saw him no more.

I turned back to my poor Winnetou, who needed me. I found him kneeling beside his father and his sister, anxiously searching for a trace of life. When he saw me coming he rose for an instant, and looked at me with an expression in his eyes I can never forget, so full of pain and wrath were they. "My brother sees what has happened. Nscho-Tschi, the fairest and best of the daughters of the Apaches, will never go to the states of the pale-faces. She still breathes, but she will never rise again."

I could not speak; I could say nothing, ask nothing. There was nothing to ask; I saw only too plainly the whole wretched truth. They lay in a pool of blood, Intschu-Tschuna shot through the head, Fair Day through the breast. He had been killed instantly; she still breathed with difficulty, and with a rattling sound, while the beautiful bronze of her face grew paler and paler. Her soft lips were drawn, and death was stamped on the dear features. She moved a little, turned her head to where her father lay, and slowly opened her eyes. She saw Intschu-Tschuna lying in his blood, and shrank at the sight, but was too weak to feel the shock keenly. She seemed to gather her thoughts together, and remember what had happened, for she pressed her little hands against her heart. She felt the warm blood flowing from her breast and sighed. "Nscho-Tschi, my dear, my only sister," moaned Winnetou, with a note in his trembling voice no words could convey. She raised her eyes to him. "Winnetou my brother," she whispered. "Avenge -- me." then she saw me, and a glad smile played over her white lips. "Shatterhand," she gasped. "You -- are -- there. Now -- I -- die -- in --" we heard no more, for death closed her lips forever. I felt as though I was suffocating; I must have air. I sprang up, for we had knelt down by her, and uttered a loud cry which echoed down the side of the mountain. Winnetou also rose, slowly, as if a heavy weight dragged him down. He threw both arms around me, and said: "Now they are dead; the greatest, noblest chief of the Apaches, and Nscho-Tschi, my sister, who loved you so. She died with your name on her lips. Never, never forget it, my dear brother."

"I will not forget it," I said hoarsely.

Then his expression changed, and he said in a voice that rang like a trumpet: "Did you hear her last words to me?"

"Yes."

"Revenge! She shall be avenged, and as no murder was ever avenged before. Do you know who the murderers are? You saw them. Pale-face, to whom we had done no wrong. So it has ever been, so will it ever be till the last red man is dead. For if he died a natural death, still it would be a murder, for his people are slain. We were going to the States of these accursed pale-faces. Nscho-Tschi wished to learn to be like the white squaws; she has paid for it with her life.

Whether we love them, or whether we hate them, it is the same. Wherever a pale-face sets his foot, destruction to us follows after him. A lament will ring through all the tribes of the Apaches, and a cry of vengeance will echo in every place where there is a son of our nation. The eyes of all the Apaches will be turned on Winnetou to see how he will avenge the death of his father and sister. My brother, Old Shatterhand, shall hear the promise I make here beside these two bodies. I swear by the Great Spirit, and by all my brave ancestors in the Happy Hunting Grounds, that with the gun which has fallen from my dead father's hand I will shoot down each and every white man I meet, or --"

"Stop!" I interrupted him, for I knew how binding and unalterable this oath would be to him. "Stop! My brother Winnetou must not swear now, not now."

"Why not?" he asked angrily.

"An oath must be spoken calmly."

"Ugh! My soul is calm now, as calm as the grave in which I shall lay my dear dead. As it will never give them back to me, so I will never take back a syllable of my oath--."

"Say no more," I interrupted him again.

His eyes flashed on me almost threateningly, and he cried: "Will Old Shatterhand hinder me doing my duty? Shall the old wives spit upon me, and shall I be driven from my people because I have not the courage to avenge today's crime?"

"It is far from my thoughts to ask this of you. I too would have the murderers punished. Three have already received their reward; the fourth has fled, but he shall not escape us."

15

"How can he escape?" Winnetou asked. "But it is not a question of him alone. He has acted like a true son of that white race which brings us ruin. It is responsible for what he has learned, and I will hold it responsible, I Winnetou now the chief of all the tribes of the Apaches."

He stood erect and proud before me, a man who, in spite of his youth, was the king of his people. Yes, he was the man to carry out whatever he undertook. He could unite the warriors of all the red nations under him, and begin a warfare on the whites which, although the end was certain, would bathe the West in the blood of a hundred thousand victims.

I took his hand, and said: "You shall do what you will, but first hear the request I make, which may be the last your white friend and brother can ask of you. Here lies Nscho-Tschi. You said that she loved me, and died with my name on her lips. And she loved you; me as friend, and you as brother, and you returned her love richly. By this our love I beg you not to take any oath as to what you will do till the stones are sealed over the grave of this worthiest daughter of the Apaches."

He looked at me earnestly, even severely, then his eyes fell, and his face softened, till at last he raised his eyes again, and said: "My brother, Old Shatterhand, has great power over all hearts around him. Nscho-Tschi would certainly do what he asked, and so will I. Not until my eyes no longer look upon these two whom we loved shall it be decided whether the Mississippi and its tributaries shall flow down to the sea red with the blood of the red and white races. I have spoken. How!"

Thank God! At least for a time I had succeeded in averting this great disaster. I pressed his hand gratefully, and said: "My brother shall see that I will ask no mercy from him for the guilty man; he may make his punishment as heavy as he deserves. We must take care he has no time to escape."

"My feet are bound," answered Winnetou, once more sad and quiet. "The customs of my people bid me remain with my dead until they are buried, because they were so closely related to me. Not until then may I seek for revenge."

"And when will they be buried?"

"I must consult my warriors whether we shall bury them here where they died, or take them back to Rio Pecos. But even if we lay them here several days must pass to celebrate fitly the burial of such a great chief."

"Then the murderer will escape."

"No, for though Winnetou cannot follow him, others can take his place. Old Shatterhand shall undertake this; he will surely find the trail of the fugitive. He shall take ten braves with him; the other twenty warriors he will send here to me to chant the death song."

"It shall be as you say, and I hope to be worthy the trust my red brother gives me."

"I know that Old Shatterhand will act exactly as if I were in his place. How!"

He gave me his hand; I pressed it in both of mine, bent once more over the faces of the dead, and went away. At the edge of the clearing I turned back. At that moment Winnetou covered his head, and uttered the dull, wailing note with which the Indians begin their death chant. Ah, how sad, how heavy-hearted that note of woe made me! But I had to act, and hastened back by the way I had come.

CHAPTER III

ON THE MURDERER'S TRACK

WHEN I left Winnetou I intended to go straight to the place where I had found Santer's horses, but on the way I thought of the horse I had ridden in coming, and that Santer must have found him, and ridden at once from the scene of his crime. This thought redoubled my speed; I ran down the mountain, and with bitter disgust saw that the horse was gone, and Santer was already on his way. I plunged through the ravine; it was too stony there to see a trail, but a little farther on I came to soft earth which I examined carefully for a footprint.

Then I found that I had been entirely deceived. Search as I would I could discover nothing; Santer had not gone this way. He must hake chosen another where the rocks betrayed no hoof prints, and the only thing for me to do was to hasten back to our camp for assistance. One person alone might spend hours in a vain attempt to discover the exit he had chosen.

It was a long distance to traverse on foot when one was on fire with impatience, grief and rage, but though it seemed to me my feet were shod with lead, in reality I was not long getting to our camp. It was past midday, however, when I came in, and Sam Hawkins called out to me as he saw me coming: "Where have you been? We have eaten, and I --"

He stopped suddenly, shocked by the expression of my face. "For the love of heaven," he cried, "what is the matter?"

Instead of answering, I called the Apaches together, and told them as well as I could my terrible news.

No one spoke or moved; they could not believe me; it was too horrible. But when they did realize I had spoken the truth, and Intschu-Tschuna and Nscho-Tschi were really dead, such a howl arose as could have been heard for miles. The Indians ran about like madmen, brandishing their tomahawks, and uttering fierce cries, their faces distorted with grief and rage.

As soon as I could make myself heard, I said: "Let the Apache braves be silent. Nothing comes of noise. We must hasten after the murderer."

"Yes; away, away, away," they shrieked, throwing themselves on their horses; had they caught Santer then he would have been torn to shreds.

"Gently," I said. "My brothers do not know what must be done; let me tell them."

They crowded around me till I was nearly suffocated, while Sam Hawkins, Stone and Parker stood as if petrified just where they were when I came back; the tragedy seemed to have benumbed them. They stirred at last, and joined us, and Sam gasped out: "I feel as though I had been knocked on the head, and could not think. The dear, beautiful, good, good young red girl! She was so friendly, so sweet to me! To think she is murdered!"

"Don't talk about it, Sam. I don't dare dwell on that side of it. Now all our strength is needed to catch that beast. My idea is to divide our force into two parties, and ride around the mountain. We will meet on the further side, and learn whether either division has found the trail. I am convinced that one or the other must find it, and then we will follow it fast."

"Upon my word the very best way, and the simplest; I wonder I didn't think of it," cried Sam.

"Winnetou has lent me ten Indians to pursue Santer, and I'll take those who are the best mounted, for no one knows how long we shall have to follow the wretch, and we must take enough provisions. You know the region; how long do you think it will take us to ride around the mountain?"

"If we hurry we can do it in a little more than two hours."

"Then let us delay no longer." I picked out my ten Apaches, who were glad to be chosen, for they much preferred hunting the murderer to singing the death song. To the remaining twenty I gave explicit directions how to reach Winnetou, and we then parted.

My ten Indians turned to the left of the mountain to encompass it on its western side, while we kept on to the east. We spurred our horses, and rode rapidly, keeping the hills on our left. Our eyes were glued to the ground, for the faster we rode the sharper we must watch not to pass the trail.

Thus we spent an hour, and half of another, and had almost finished our half circuit of the hills when we spied a dark line running through the grass. It was the trail of a single rider -- Santer's. It was not more than two hours old, and we longed to follow it at once, but had to wait for the Apaches, who came up with us in three-quarters of an hour.

I sent a man back to Winnetou to tell him that we had found the trail, and then we rode on at our best speed. It was so early in the season that there were but two hours before sunset, and we must hasten. We must put a long stretch behind us before darkness came on, for we could not see the trail during the night. We felt sure that Santer would press on in the darkness, knowing well we must be following, and tomorrow our ride would be a long one. Fortunately, however, both horse and man would require rest; Santer could not ride forever without stopping.

Nugget Mountain disappeared behind us, and a flat prairie lay before us, in which the trail was easily seen. As it grew dark we dismounted, and followed it on foot until we could distinguish it no longer. There was grass here for the horses, and we lay down for the night just as we were. The thought of the death of Intschu-Tschuna and his daughter kept my eyes open, and when I closed them I saw them lying in their blood, and heard again Nscho-Tschi's dying words. I reproached myself for not showing how fully I appreciated the love and kindness they had shown me, and felt as wretched as if my own hand had slain them. It grew cold toward morning, and we were so chilled that we started out while it was still gray dawn, and the trail was scarcely discernible. Our horses too were cold, and needed no other spur to speed.

We rode east till mid-day, when the trail turned more toward the south. Sam Hawkins noticed this, and looked thoughtful. "This fellow is deep," he said. "I believe he's gone to the Kiowas."

"He'd never do that!"

"Why not? Do you think he'd stand still for love of you, and let you have his head? He'll do his best to save himself. He had his eyes open, and saw our horses were better than his, and he's afraid he can't hold out, so he'll seek the Kiowas' protection. They'll do anything for him when he tells them he has killed Intschu-Tschuna and Nscho-Tschi."

It was not long after that we came to the place where Santer had rested. We saw that his horse had lain down; he was very tired, as the trail had already shown. Apparently the rider was worn out too, for the trail from this point was not more than two hours old; he had probably slept longer than he intended. We were a good half hour nearer him than we had been the day before. The trail stretched still more to the south, and we steadily gained on him; it could not now be more than half an hour old. The horizon before us was dark; there was no longer open prairie, but woods ahead of us.

Just before evening we were so close to the fugitive that we might discover him at any moment, and we pressed forward more eagerly than ever. We rode through one of the groups of trees that stood on the left bank of a little stream. I was ahead, and as I passed the last tree I saw that the trail led into the dry bed of the brook. I reined up for a moment to tell this to the others, which was fortunate for us, for in that moment of delay I followed the bed of the little stream with my eye, and made a discovery which caused me to conceal myself hastily.

On the opposite bank of the stream there was a second piece of woods which was alive with Indians and their horses; I could see the stakes in the ground, across which they had stretched ropes to dry their meat. Had I ridden fifteen feet further they would have seen me. I dismounted and pointed out the scene to my companions. "Kiowas!" said one of the Apaches.

"Yes, Kiowas," assented Sam. "The devil must love this Santer to have given him this protection at the last moment. I actually felt him between my fingers, but even now he shan't escape."

"It's not a strong force of Kiowas," I said.

"H'm. We see only those who are under those trees. You don't know how many more there are. They're hunting, and are drying their meat."

I wanted to go back further from the Kiowa camp where we would be in less danger of discovery, but Sam laughed at me, assuring me we were as safe there as if we were in New York. He frequently called me rash and foolhardy, but now the roles were reversed, and he insisted on a risk I was most unwilling to run. He was entirely unlike himself in every way that day; the death of the "dear, beautiful, good young red girl" had made him half insane with rage. In this case, though, the Apaches, as well as Stone and Parker agreed with him, so I reluctantly gave way to such a majority, and we tied our horses, and sat down where we were to wait for darkness. The Kiowas evidently felt perfectly secure; they rode and walked across the open plain, called to one another, and in every way behaved as if they were in their own well-guarded Indian village.

"You see how unsuspecting they are," said Sam.

"If things are as they seem," I returned. "But I have a presentiment they are fooling us."

"Presentiment! Only old women have presentiments; no one else. What object could they have in fooling us?"

"To draw us on."

"That's quite unnecessary, for we'll go on without drawing. Santer is over there, and has told them the whole story. They know of course we'll follow him, bet they don't think we're as near as we are; they're probably looking for us in the morning. As soon as it's dark I'll crawl over there and spy on them, and then we'll know what to do."

"Good. I'll go too."

"You needn't. When Sam Hawkins goes spying he doesn't need help," he said so curtly, and with an irritation so unlike his usual jolly self that I made no reply, understanding that he was not only saddened by the death of our friends, but angry and sore that his own imprudent talkativeness on the day we met Santer had probably caused all the trouble. I stretched myself out as though consenting to Sam's will, and was silent.

The sun had been down some time, and now the twilight too faded. The legion fires burned brightly, and it was so unlike Indians to thus carelessly announce their presence to a possible enemy that this confirmed my previous opinion of their game. While I lay thinking this over it seemed to me I heard a rustle behind me, where none of our people lay. I listened, and the sound was repeated; I heard it plainly, and could distinguish exactly what it was. The light movement of dried vines rubbing against each other. It might be caused by some little animal, but it might be caused by a man; I must look into it. I rose, and strolled in the opposite direction from whence the sound came. When I had gone far enough, I turned and crept around on the other side. I heard the noise again; crawled up, and saw exactly what I expected to see -- an Indian who had been hidden there, and was trying to get away noiselessly, but was caught in the blackberry vines. He had almost freed himself; his body was out, except one shoulder and arm, and the neck and head. I crept up behind his back. He gradually got out all but his arm, when I rose to my knees -- I had been lying flat -- caught him around the neck with my left arm, and dealt two -- three stunning blows on his head which laid him motionless.

"What was that?" said Sam.

"Did you hear anything?"

"Old Shatterhand's horse stamped," said Dick.

"He's gone; where can he be? He'll do something foolish," cried Sam.

"Foolish? Not he. He never was yet, and he won't be now." I rose, and went softly over to them, and said: "You're mistaken, dear Sam. I haven't gone away. But if you want proof that I was right about the Kiowas, go over to those blackberry vines."

He rose, mystified. "Hallo!" he cried. "Why, it's an Indian. How did this happen?"

"He was hidden in the blackberry brambles, and I discovered him. He was trying to get out when I knocked him senseless. That was what you heard when you thought my horse was restless."

"Confound it! He has been spying. How lucky he didn't get back to his own gang. Bind him, and gag him. I'm going over now to spy on them. You stay here!"

He started at once, and the Apaches murmured at his ordering me so peremptorily, and Stone said: "Well, I really don't know what's come over Sam."

"Never mind; he's all right," I said. "He's a good, faithful little fellow, but he's half crazed by the murder, and the thought that it was he who gave Santer the fatal information. Of course I am going over there, though. You stay here till I come back; even if you hear shots don't come unless I call you."

I laid my gun down, and started. Sam had gone one way; not the best one, I thought, so I took the other, intending to creep up on the opposite side. I made my way successfully, and found myself under the trees where the thick darkness of the wood was increased by the contrast of the light of eight fires which the Kiowas were burning, although I counted but twenty Indians around them. They were evidently intended as decoys for us. The Kiowas had their guns in their hands ready to shoot at an instant, and woe to us if we had accepted their cordial invitation to fall on them. I crept from tree to tree, till at last I saw Santer. He was sitting with four Indians, and to my delight they were talking in perfectly audible tones. I heard Santer holding forth. He told them of Nugget Mountain, and urged the Indians to go there with him to get the treasure.

"Does my white brother know the place where it is?" asked the oldest of the four Indians. "No; we should have learned, but the Apaches came back too soon. We thought they would be so long that we could spy upon them."

"Then is the search nearly hopeless. Ten times a hundred men could go there, and look carefully, and find nothing. The red men know well how to make such places undiscoverable. But since my brother has killed the greatest of our enemies and his daughter, we will go with him later, and help him seek. But first we must capture your pursuers, and kill Winnetou."

"Winnetou! He will be with them."

"No; for he may not leave his dead, and he will keep the greater part of his braves with him. He has sent the smaller part after you, and they will probably be led by Old Shatterhand, the white dog who shot our chief, Tangua, in both knees over in the Apache pueblo. It is his band that we are now waiting for."

"Then we will ride over to Nugget Mountain, lay Winnetou out cold, and get the gold."

"That is not as easy as my Brother thinks. Winnetou has to bury his father and sister, and we could not kill him before that was done, for the Great Spirit would never forgive us. But when they are buried we will fall upon him. He will not go to the States of the pale-faces now, but will return to Rio Pecos. We will lay a trap for him as we have today for Old Shatterhand, who is surely over yonder. I only wait for the return of the spy I have sent there. It is strange that the sentries I have posted over toward them send me no tidings yet."

I was alarmed as I heard these words; there were sentinels then on the outskirts of the woods. Suppose Sam Hawkins did not see them, and fell into their hands! Scarcely had this thought come to me than I heard a short, sharp cry. The Kiowa leader sprang up, and listened, as did all the Indians. Four Kiowas came out of the woods bringing a white man, who struggled to no purpose, for though he was not bound, four knives would have pierced him had he broken away. This white man was my short-sighted Sam Hawkins! My resolution was quickly taken; I would not let him be killed, though I risked my life to prevent it.

"Sam Hawkins!" cried Santer, recognizing him. "Good evening, sir. You did not expect to see me here."

"Beast! thief! Murderer!" cried the fearless little Sam, springing at his throat as the Indians released him. "I've got you now, and you shall have your pay."

The murderer defended himself, and the Indians pulled Sam off. Confusion reigned for a moment, and I made the most of it. Drawing my two revolvers I sprang out. "Old Shatterhand!" cried Santer, starting to run.

I sent two shots after him, which failed their mark, emptied the other barrels among the Indians, and cried to Sam: "Come away; get behind me." for a moment the Indians seemed unable to move. I seized Sam's arm, and drew him into the woods. It was all done so quickly that scarcely more than a minute had passed since I had jumped out." mercy on us, that was none too soon," said Sam as we passed into the shadow.

"Don't talk; follow me," I interrupted, letting go his arm, and turning up the stream to get as far away as possible before attempting to cross, intending to come down behind our camp. When I thought we had gone far enough to be secure, I paused. "Sam," I said, softly. No answer. "Sam, do you hear me?" I asked louder. Still no answer. Where could he be? Had he not followed me? I took cartridges from my belt, reloaded my revolvers, and turned back to seek him. I went slowly, step by step, till I reached the spot where I had called on him to follow me. He must have disregarded my call, and tried to cross where he was; if this were so then the firelight must have fallen on him, and he had placed himself directly in the range of the Kiowa bullets. What carelessness on the part of the little man, so obstinate today! I went up the stream again, crossed out of sight, and reached our camp, where I found everything in good order. My red and white comrades pressed around me, thankful to see me safe, and I asked at once: "Where is Sam? Isn't he here?"

"How can you ask?" said Stone." didn't you see what happened to him?"

"What?"

"Sam appeared right over there, and there was a crowd of Kiowas after him. They captured him, and were off to the other side, and disappeared under the trees before we could get to the spot. We wanted to go after them and rescue Sam, but we remembered you had bade us stay here, and obeyed."

"That was wise, for twelve men could do nothing in that crowd but be killed."

"But what shall we do? Sam is a prisoner."

"Yes, and for the second time."

I then told them what had happened, and as I concluded Will Parker said: "It's no fault of yours. You have done more than another would have dared do. Sam's crazy today, and has only himself to blame. But we can't leave him there."

"No; wait till things quiet down a bit, and then we'll crawl over to see what can be done."

Two hours later, having made sure our horses were fast, and our prisoner safely bound and gagged, we crept over, Will and I, to spy upon our foe. We found the fires burning as brightly as before, but not a soul beside them. The Kiowas had silently slipped away. The dawn showed us their trail leading in the direction of the Kiowa village. Stone and Parker were beside themselves at the thought that Sam had been taken away to torture, but I reminded them that we had a hostage in our Kiowa prisoner, and furthermore I felt sure they were not bound for their own village, but for Nugget Mountain, to capture Winnetou as soon as the burial was over. There was nothing for us to do but make our best speed back to warn him, and we set forth very ill pleased with the result of our ride, not having captured Santer, and having lost Sam Hawkins.

It was noon of the second day when we passed through the ravine, and found ourselves back on the scene of the double murder. We saw at once how busy the twenty Apaches whom we left with Winnetou had been. They had built the tomb, and the burial was to be on the next day. Winnetou was told we had come, and came out from beside his dead to greet us. He was always grave, and rarely laughed; I never heard him laugh aloud, but there was an expression of kindliness in his gravity, and his eyes were smiling and friendly. But today his face seemed turned to stone, and there was no light in his eyes. His movements were slow and painful as he came toward me, took my hand, and looked at me long and earnestly.

"When did my brother come back?" he asked.

"Just now."

"Where is the murderer?"

"He has escaped."

I confess that my eyes fell as I made this answer, and I felt ashamed to give it. His eyes too sought the ground. After a long pause he asked: "Did my brother lose the trail?"

"No, I have it still. He is coming here."

"Let Old Shatterhand tell me all." he seated himself on a stone, and I sat beside him to tell him the whole unsatisfactory story.

He listened in silence to the end, and then pressed my hand, and said: "My brother will forgive me asking if he had lost the trail. He has done all that could be done, and has acted with great wisdom. Sam Hawkins will deeply repent his imprudence; we will forgive him, and free him. I think, as my brother does, that the Kiowas will come, but they will not find us unprepared. Tomorrow we will seal the tomb over Intschu-Tschuna and Nscho-Tschi. Will my brother be there?"

"I should be deeply grieved if Winnetou would not allow me to be there."

"I do not only allow it, but I beg you to be there. Your presence may perhaps save the lives of many sons of the pale-faces. The law of blood demands the death of many white men, but your eyes are like the sun whose warmth melts the hard ice, and turns it into running water. You know what I have lost; I am alone. Be to me father and sister, I pray you, Jack." tears stood in his eyes; he was ashamed of them, and hastened back to his dead.

We buried the chief and his young daughter on the following day. Interesting as were the ceremonies, I cannot describe them, for when I think of that sorrowful hour my heart is as full of pain as if it were yesterday. Intschu-Tschuna's body was bound on his horse, which was strapped to the ground so that it could not move, and then shot through the head. The earth was piled over them until horse and rider, with his medicine charms and his weapons, were completely covered, and then they were built around with stone, and the tomb sealed.

At my request Nscho-Tschi received another kind of grave; I could not bear to have the earth heaped on her sweet face and kind hands. We seated her against the trunk of a tree, and built a stone pyramid around her, from the top of which the green branches of the tree waved in the soft southern wind.

CHAPTER IV

PLANS FAIL ON BOTH SIDES

WINNETOU's hour of mourning was past. Before, and during the burial of the father and sister who were so dear to him he gave himself up to the pain of their loss but that over he was no longer the son and brother, but the leader of his warriors, the avenger of their murder, and turned all his attention to the expected coming of the Kiowas. He was ready with a plan, and as soon as the last stone was placed over his dead he bade the Apaches bring the horses from the valley up the mountain.

"Why does my brother give this order?" I asked. "The way is so hard that it will be a great effort to bring the horses up here."

"I know," he replied "but it must be done, because I mean to entrap the Kiowas. They have protected the murderer, and must all die -- all!"

His face looked so stern and resolute as he said this that I knew if his plan succeeded the Kiowas were lost. I was inclined to milder counsels; they were our enemies, of course, but they were not guilty of the death of Intschu-Tschuna and Nscho-Tschi. Dared I oppose him? I might draw down his anger on myself, but it was a favorable opportunity for such a plea because we were alone, and no one would be the wiser if he gave me an angry answer, while if one of the Indians was by to hear it I should have to resent it. So I gently gave my opinion on the matter, and to my surprise it had not the effect I dreaded. He looked at me with great gloomy eyes, but said quietly: "I might have looked for this from my brother; he does not consider it a weakness to spare an enemy."

"I do not mean that; there can be no question of sparing them. I have been thinking how to capture them. But they are not guilty of the crime committed here, and it would be unjust to punish them for it."

"They have harbored the murderer, and are coming here to capture us. Is not that reason enough that they should die?"

"No; not for me at least. It grieves me to see that my brother Winnetou falls into the same mistake that all the red men make."

"What mistake does Old Shatterhand mean?"

"That the Indians destroy one another, instead of uniting against the common foe. Let me be frank with you. Who do you think is stronger and wiser, the red man or the white man?"

"The pale-face. I say this because it is true. They have more knowledge and skill than we, and surpass us in every way."

"That is so. We do surpass the Indian, but you are not an ordinary Indian. The Great Spirit has given you gifts rarely found among the pale-faces, and therefore I would not have you think and act like an ordinary red man. How often is the war hatchet dug up between the tribes! Your eyes are keener than these warriors' eyes; you must see it is suicide for the red men to turn on one another. Intschu-Tschuna and Nscho-Tschi were murdered, not by a red man, but by a white, and because he fled to the Kiowas, and urged them to come here and capture you, you would shoot them down like dogs. They are your red brothers; consider that."

I talked in this strain to him for some time, and at last Winnetou gave me his hand, saying: "Old Shatterhand is a sincere friend of all red men. He is right when he speaks of suicide. I will do as he wishes; I will take the Kiowas prisoners, but I will spare them, and be satisfied to keep Santer in my hands."

"I thank you. My brother Winnetou has a heart open to all that is good. Perhaps he will be as merciful in another regard."

"What does my brother Old Shatterhand mean?"

"You would have sworn vengeance on all the white race, and I begged you to wait till after the burial. May I ask what you have decided upon?"

He dropped his eyes to the ground for a while, then looking me full in the face, pointed to the temporary hut where the dead had lain, and said: "I struggled with myself all night long there beside my dead. I had thought of a tremendous revenge. I would call together all the tribes of the red nation, and lead them against the pale-faces. I was in a combat, but in this combat against myself I was victorious."

"Then you have abandoned this plan?"

"Yes. I have asked three persons whom I loved, two dead and one living, what I should do. They bade me give up my plan, and I will do as they bid me."

I looked the question I did not ask, and he added: "My brother does not know of whom I speak? Kleki-Petrah, my white teacher who died for me, Nscho-Tschi, and you are the ones I mean whom I questioned in thought, and they all gave me the same answer."

"I am thankful that my brother Winnetou came to this decision. First of all it is right, and then such an attack on the whites could have ended only in misfortune for you."

"I know. The white men are so many that they would have sent new forces against us every day, while we could not renew our warriors. I thought of all this during the night as I sat by my dead, and gave up my plan, deciding to be satisfied with wreaking my vengeance on the murderer, and his friends. But now my brother, Old Shatterhand, has spoken against this, and my vengeance shall only be in punishing Santer."

"These words make me proud of the friendship that unites us. I will not forget what you have done. And now we are both sure that the Kiowas are coming but we know not when, and even if we did it will be hard to overcome a force so much larger than ours."

"They will come today," Winnetou said as positively as if he saw them advancing. "And as to the rest, we will get them in a place where they cannot defend themselves."

"That was my own idea, but is there such a place?"

"Yes, there is a rocky ravine near by; I will trap my enemies there. The Kiowas have sent Sam Hawkins to their village; they will not bring him here, and those who took him back have summoned the warriors from the village to attack us. This has delayed them; they have not yet reached the foot of the mountain, but they will surely be here today."

"How do you know they are not yet in the valley?"

Winnetou pointed to the top of the next mountain; it was crowned with woods, out of which rose one very tall tree. It was the highest point of these hills, and any one who had good eyes and sat in that tree could overlook the entire surrounding country.

"My brother does not know," said Winnetou, "that I sent a brave there who will see the Kiowas coming, for he has the eye of a hawk. As soon as they come he will warn me. They will be here today, for they will not dare delay longer, if they wish to take us."

"They did not intend coming to Nugget Mountain, but meant to capture us on our way home."

"And they might have succeeded had you not heard their plans, but now I know them I will draw the Kiowas after me by going in the opposite direction from our pueblo."

"If they only follow you!"

"They will. In any case they must send a spy to discover where we are. That is why I had the horses brought here. There are thirty-six beasts, and though the ground is rocky, they must see their trail, and follow us. We will go from here into the ravine which is to be their trap. We shall not go deep into it, for the spy will only follow us far enough to make sure we are really there, and then he will go back to tell his chief we are not gone southward, but northward. Does my brother agree to this?"

"Yes; it will force them to alter their plans, and we can wait, certain that they will come after us here."

"They will; I am sure of it. Santer will be in my hands today."

At this moment the horses were brought up, mine, and Sam's long-eared Nancy, the mule, among the rest. We could not mount, for the way was too rough to ride, so we each took a bridle, and led the horses up the difficult pass. Winnetou went ahead, leading us northward till we came to an open plain where we could mount, and we rode toward the side of another mountain which rose before us like a high, perpendicular wall. It was cleft by a small ravine to which Winnetou pointed, saying: "That is the trap of which I spoke." the word trap suited well the narrow opening into which we now passed. If the Kiowas were so foolish as to follow us here, and we were stationed at the only exit of the ravine, it would be utter madness for them to think of making any resistance.

The path did not run straight, but turned from left to right, and we were a good quarter of an hour reaching the exit. There we dismounted and had scarcely done so before we saw coming toward us the Apache who had been watching for the Kiowas from the high tree.

"They are coming," he said. "I wanted to count them, but could not, because they rode single file, and were too far away."

"Did they turn toward the valley?" asked Winnetou.

"No; they went straight to the place where they camped the other night. A single brave came out from them on foot, and I saw him go toward the valley."

"That is the spy. We have just time to bait our trap. My brother Shatterhand may take Stone and Parker, and twelve of my braves, and go around the mountain to the left. When he reaches a very strong, tall birch tree let him turn into the woods. When he has done this my brother will soon find himself in the extension of that valley from which we ascended to Nugget Mountain. Going on through the valley he will come to the place where we left our horses; the rest of the way he knows. He must not go into the valley, but must stay hidden on its side in the woods. He will observe the enemies' spies, but will not oppose them. Then he will see the enemy coming, and let them enter the ravine."

"So that is your plan?" I said. "You stay here to keep the exit to the ravine, and I go around to wait for the Kiowas, then follow them secretly till they are in the trap?"

"Yes, that is my plan, and if my brother is cautious it will succeed. But hasten; the afternoon is almost over, and the Kiowas will do what they have to do today."

The sun had almost finished its course; the evening would be on us in little more than an hour. I started at once with the companions Winnetou had appointed me, on foot, of course. We reached the birch tree in a short quarter of an hour, and turned into the woods. We found each landmark as Winnetou had described it, and reached the place where we were to halt. The Apaches were perfectly silent; Stone and Parker spoke together softly at first, but soon their whispering ceased. A breeze played over the tree tops with that monotonous rustle, which is not a rustle, but an uninterrupted, deep and slow sigh, so easily distinguished from all other rustling. And with that I heard another sound. I listened more keenly; something moved. What was it? An animal would not have ventured so near us. A reptile? No, not that. I turned over quickly on the other side where I could see better under the trees, and could just distinguish a dark object slipping away between them. I sprang toward it. It looked like a dark shadow before me. I made a grab for it, and got a piece of cloth in my hand.

"Get out," cried a startled voice, and the cloth was torn from me, the shadow was no more to be seen.

My comrades sprang up, asking what had happened.

"Be still, be still," I said, and listened. Nothing was to be heard. It was a man who had been spying on us, probably Santer from the English exclamation. I ground my teeth as I thought the villain had been so near.

"Sit down, and wait till I come back," I said to my followers, and rushed through the woods. I could see no one, but I would go to the edge of the valley where the man must come out to get back to the Kiowas, and seize him. This was a beautiful plan, but it could not be carried out, for as I followed the bend of the valley I saw men and horses before me, and had to turn back hastily under the trees, for I had come out right on the Kiowa camp. Evidently Santer had ridden ahead of the Indians to see if it was safe for them to approach, and as he had not returned they had sent the Indian spy to discover why. The Kiowas would not fall into our hands to-night, or the next day either if Santer had been clever enough to discover our plans. What was to be done? Should I wait at my post to see if the Kiowas fell into our trap? Should I go to Winnetou and tell him of my discovery? Or should I try to spy on the Kiowas in my turn? The latter course was very dangerous, but it would be of incalculable value to us to learn their plans. I risked much, everything, in trying it, but I decided to venture. They burned no fire, and that fact served me as well as them. Under the trees there was a high rock, overgrown with moss, and surrounded by ferns; perhaps I could hide behind it. Lying flat on the ground I wriggled in that direction.

It had grown so dark that it was not necessary to seek cover; I could be discovered only if one of the Indians came that way, and stumbled over me, and luckily this did not happen. The Indians talked together in low tones, yet I could hear every word, only unfortunately I did not understand their dialect.

I may have lain behind the rock ten minutes when I heard the sentinel challenge, and the answer I longed for came: "It is I -- Santer."

The chief called him over to himself, and he sat down where I could almost touch him.

"My white brother has been much longer than we agreed; he must have had an important reason for this," said the chief.

"More important than you imagine," answered Santer. I could follow the conversation now, for with Santer the Indians spoke the jargon used with the whites.

27

"Let my white brother tell me what he has seen and heard."

Santer obeyed this request. I listened eagerly while he repeated to the Kiowas all the conversation between Winnetou and me beside the graves, including the smallest details of our plans. The cunning beast had been near us then, had spied upon us step by step till he knew our very thoughts. As he ended he told the Indians that I, with two white men and something over ten Apaches, was above in the woods guarding the entrance to the ravine. "I lay so close behind Old Shatterhand that I could almost touch him," he concluded. "Wouldn't he be furious if he knew it?" he was right. My hands were cut by my nails as I clenched them, longing to throttle him, and not daring to move.

Truly this man was as cunning and bold as he was wicked. Poor Sam was right when he said the devil must love him well. If I could have only held him when I had him by the coat! If I had, the whole history of Winnetou's life would have been changed, and he might have been here now. So man's fate hangs on a brief moment, on a trivial action, but we do not know what is best, and the great Ruler of the universe, without whose consent no little leaf grows green, or fades, watches over His children.

There was one consolation for me; only one. I was now spying on Santer as he had spied on us, and the end was not yet. If I listened eagerly before, I now strained my ears as the question came up as to the best move for the Kiowas to make under the circumstances. The Indians wished to go back toward their village, feeling sure that Winnetou would follow to free Sam Hawkins, and capture Santer. This was against the wishes of that precious rascal, who was not inclined to take any such risks as lurked in this change of plan, although the Kiowas so far outnumbered us. He insisted that I and my companions must first be attacked and captured, and then Winnetou and his Apaches marched on, and surprised. He felt sure that he could successfully lead the Kiowas on me first, and then on Winnetou in the dark. Though he was more than willing that I should be shot at once, he wanted of all things to capture Winnetou alive, since he alone could tell the hiding-place of the treasure in the mountain, a secret he purposed extracting from the young Apache by torture. The leader of the Kiowa band opposed this counsel at first, but by strong arguments, and appeal to the probable displeasure of his chief if he let slip a chance to attack us when our force was divided and weakened, Santer brought him to his way of thinking.

I only waited to hear that this would be done at once, and slipped away into the woods, for it was high time I was off. As soon as I was far enough back to risk it, I rose and ran as fast as I could by the starlight glimmering through the trees, back to my comrades.

"Who comes here?" cried Dick Stone. "Is that you, Jack?"

"Yes."

"How long you were. Who was hidden there? An Indian, I suppose."

"No; Santer!"

"Santer! Good heavens! And we didn't catch him!"

"We've no time to talk; we must get out of here as quick as we can. The Kiowas are coming to capture us."

"Are you joking?"

"No. I've been listening to them. We're to be caught right away, and Winnetou in the morning. They know our plan. Hurry up; we've got to warn Winnetou. Hurry, I say."

We went in the darkness through the pathless forest. Our eyes had to be in our fingers, for the sense of touch, and not sight had to guide us. At last we reached Winnetou's camping place. He had stationed sentinels even on the side whence we came, which was not likely to be approached. The sentinel challenged us in a loud voice, and I answered as loudly. He recognized my voice, and sprang up, while Winnetou asked wonderingly: "My brother comes? What has happened? We have waited in vain for the Kiowas."

"They are coming in the morning, not by the ravine, but up the side of the mountain to capture you."

"Ugh! This could only be if they knew our plan."

"They do know it."

"Impossible!"

"Indeed they do. Santer was over there by the graves, and heard all you said to me when we were alone."

I could not see his face, but the profound silence in which he received this piece of news showed how amazed and angry he was. Then he seated himself, and made a place for me beside him, while the Apaches crowded around not to lose a word of my story.

"If you know this you must have spied on him, as he did on us," said Winnetou, trying to find some consolation.

"Certainly."

"Then we are quits. Tell us all that has happened."

My story was interrupted by an occasional "Ugh!" of surprise from the Apaches, but Winnetou was silent till I had finished, then he said: "My brother acted precisely as I would have done were I in his place. What does he advise us now?"

"We must capture Santer, and free Sam Hawkins."

"Yes. Our way from here lies toward the Kiowa village, but it need not be the same road the Kiowas take."

"Does my brother know where Tangua, the Kiowa chief's village lies?"

"As well as I know where my own pueblo is. It is in the Salt Fork of the Red River."

"In a southerly direction from here then?"

"Yes"

"Then let us go northwesterly from here, and come down on them from the opposite direction."

"That is precisely what I would do. My brother's thoughts are as mine. It is as my father Intschu-Tschuna said when we drank one another's blood in the bond of brotherhood. 'Life dwells in the blood. The souls of these two young warriors shall be united into a single soul. Old Shatterhand's thoughts shall be the thoughts of Winnetou, and what Winnetou wills that shall be Old Shatterhand's will." Thus did he speak. His eye looked into our hearts, and read our future. It will rejoice him in the Happy Hunting Grounds, and increase his bliss to see his words fulfilled. How!

He was silent, and all who were around him respected the tribute he was paying to the memory of his good father.

CHAPTER V

RESCUING SAM

WINNETOU threw off the remembrance of his sorrow with a sigh, and said to me: "Will my brother come with me to a place where when day breaks we can watch the opening of the ravine, and learn whether or not the Kiowas leave here? It may be that not finding Old Shatterhand, they will go back to their village, without trying to capture us in the morning. It is most important for us to watch their movements."

"Is there a place where we can see the mouth of the ravine?"

"I know such a place. Let my brothers take their horses by the bridles and follow me."

We did as he bade us, and after we had gone some hundred feet we came to a great group of trees, behind which we made another halt. Here we could camp without being discovered if the Kiowas came upon us in the night. The ravine lay directly within range, and when morning came we could see all that happened there.

The night was as cold as the previous one had been. I waited till my horse lay down, then lay myself in the hollow of his neck that he might warm me, and the beast kept as still as if he had understood the service required of him.

As the gray dawn lifted we scanned the ravine carefully for more than an hour. Nothing was to be seen there, so we decided to find out where the Kiowas were. I suggested to Winnetou that if we went over to the spot from which the Apache spy had discovered them yesterday, we must see whether they had gone away or not. This suggestion Winnetou approved, and we acted on it at once.

When we reached the southern side of Nugget Mountain we found two broad, clear trails, one of yesterday leading into the valley, and a fresh one leading away from it. That the Kiowas were gone there could no longer be a doubt. They had carefully made their trail unusually plain, hoping that we would follow after them, but a scornful little smile played on Winnetou's lips as he looked at it, and he said: "These Kiowas meant to act very wisely, and they have done precisely the reverse. Such a trail as this would naturally arouse our suspicion, and we should be most foolish if we followed it."

As we had already decided, we rode away in the opposite direction, intending to descend on the Kiowa village on the unprotected side. We reached the North Fork of the Red River on the next day. The water was low, but the banks were green, and afforded much needed fodder for our horses. The Salt Fork flows from the west into the Red River, south of the North Fork, and in the junction of this arm with the main stream lay the Kiowa village of which Tangua was chief. We rode straight down toward it, traveling in the night to be cautious, and early in the morning we saw the river lying before us. We were on the wrong side of the stream, and Winnetou and I left our people encamped, and rode down further, looking for a place where we could cross with less danger of betraying our camp than if we went over directly in front of it, where our trail would lead straight to it. This care in concealing our trail cost time, but the wisdom of it was proved sooner than we expected.

We had not got back to the river, but were still on the prairie, when we saw two riders with fully a dozen pack horses coming straight toward us. One rode before, the other behind their well-laden beasts, and though we could not see their faces, their clothing was that of white men. The indications were that they had come from the Kiowa village, and we might learn something important from them. Therefore I asked Winnetou if we should not speak to them.

"Yes," he replied. "But they must not know who we are. They are pale-faces; pedlars who have been trading with the Kiowas."

"Very well. I am employed by an Indian agency, and am bound to the Kiowas on agency business. I do not understand their speech, so have taken you along. You are a Pawnee Indian."

"That is very good; my brother may speak with these two pale-faces."

We rode up to them. They raised their guns as is customary in the Far West when a stranger appears, and thus awaited our coming.

"Put down your weapons, friends," I cried when we were within hailing distance. "We won't eat you."

"It would be well for you not to try; we can bite too," one of them replied. "You strike us as doubtful characters."

"Doubtful? Why, pray?"

"Well, when two men, one white and the other red, wander around the prairies alone they are usually robbers. And your clothes are rather Indian-like. Naturally we suspect you."

"Thanks for your frankness. It is always good to know how one strikes others. But I assure you, you are quite mistaken."

"Possibly. You haven't a rogue's face, that's a fact. Perhaps you won't mind telling us where you come from."

"Not in the least. We come from beyond Washita, and are bound for the Kiowa village where Tangua is chief."

"Well, if you take my advice you'll turn round and go back, and not let a Kiowa catch sight of you. This Tangua has taken the praiseworthy resolution of killing every white man who falls into his hands, and every Indian who isn't a Kiowa. How do you happen to have this Indian with you?"

"Because I don't understand the Kiowa dialect; he is my interpreter, a Pawnee."

"Well, if you both want to be tortured to death, ride on, and you'll get your desire. Tangua has a prisoner now waiting that fate, one of Old Shatterhand's men. The Kiowas are going to capture him next, with the young Apache chief, Winnetou. This prisoner they've caught is a queer customer, who laughs all the time, and doesn't act as though death waited him."

"Have you seen him?"

"I saw him when he was brought in, and lay fastened, on the ground for an hour. Then he was taken to the island."

"An island which serves as prison?"

"Yes; it lies in the Salt Fork, some feet from the village, and is well guarded."

"Did you speak to this prisoner?"

"A few words. I asked him if I could do anything for him. He smiled at me in a friendly way, and said he dearly loved buttermilk, and if I were riding to Cincinnati he'd be much obliged if I'd bring him a glass. He's an absurd fellow. He won't be badly treated just now, though, for Old Shatterhand has a Kiowa prisoner as hostage. Only Santer exerts himself to make his life a burden to him."

"Santer! That's the name of a white man! Are there other whites among the Kiowas?"

31

"Only this one called Santer; a fellow that's most repulsive to me."

"Is he the chief's guest, or has he a separate tent?"

"He has one to himself, and not one like the chief's, such as they give a welcome guest, but an old leather hut quite at the end of the village. It seems to me he's not in high favor with Tangua either."

"Can't you describe this Santer's tent to me exactly?"

"What's the use? You'll be sure to see it when you get there. It's the fourth or fifth, counting up the stream. I don't believe you'll want to see much of him; he has a villain's face; look out for him. In spite of your dignity, you're still very young, and won't mind a bit of advice. Now I must go on. Goodbye. I hope you'll get out with a whole skin."

"Thank you. Oh, could you tell me the name of this white prisoner?"

"Sam Hawkins, and he's a well-known trapper in spite of his absurdity. I was sorry not to be able to help him. Possibly the chief would listen to you more favorably than he did to me if you speak a word for him."

"I'll try it. Goodbye."

"We have learned enough," said Winnetou, as the honest fellows rode on. "We know nearly exactly where Sam Hawkins is, and also which is Santer's tent, and we will find them both. We will ride on till these traders are out of sight, and then go back to our camp."

The traders' forms gradually grew dimmer in the distance; they had to ride slowly because their horses were so laden. As soon as they had disappeared, we turned back, carefully obliterating our tracks, and reached our camp safely. Dick Stone and Will Parker were delighted at getting tidings of their little Sam; the Apaches rejoiced that Santer was waiting them, and everybody bestirred himself energetically in breaking up our present camp, and following Winnetou to an island where we should be more securely hidden than in our present position.

We made ourselves comfortable in the new quarters, and went to sleep, knowing that there would be no rest for us in the coming night. When it was dark we were wakened to set out for the village. We laid aside all but the necessary clothing, and for weapons carried only our knives. Then we jumped into the river, and swam up stream for an hour, when we came to the place where the Salt Fork flows into Red River, and had but to follow the former a few feet before we saw the lights of the fires in the village, which lay on the left bank.

A fire burned before each tent, at which the occupants sat warming themselves and preparing their supper. The largest tent stood in the middle of the village. Its entrance was adorned with spears and eagle feathers. At the fire before this tent sat Tangua, the chief, with a young Indian perhaps eighteen years old, and two younger boys. "Those are his sons," said Winnetou. "The oldest is his favorite, and will be a brave warrior. His speed is so great that he is called Pida, which means *The Deer*."

I looked around for the island. The heavens were overcast, and no stars were shining, but the fire enabled us to see the islands lying at short distances from one another.

"There at the further end of the village, in the fourth or fifth tent, is Santer," whispered Winnetou. "We will not keep together. I must go to hunt up the dwelling of the murderer of my father and sister, and spy on him. You seek Sam, who is your comrade."

"And where shall we meet again?"

"Here, where we separate, or wait, that may be impossible. If you come through this safely, go back to our camp, but by an indirect way, not to betray the direction of our flight."

"Good! And if anything goes wrong with you, I will come to you."

Even as I spoke Winnetou was gone, creeping toward the tent where lay the wretch who had done him such great wrong.

I swam up stream under water, and came up to breathe at the upper end of the first island. Sam was not here, but indications pointed toward his being on the second one, the approach to which was going to be easier than I had feared. There were a great many canoes tied to the shore, and they would afford me a shelter under which I could swim up and see the entire island.

As I lay under one of the canoes, trying in vain to get a glimpse of the prisoner and his guard, I heard a rustle above me; it was Pida, the "deer," coming in a canoe. Luckily he landed above me, and presently I heard voices; one was my good old Sam's; the other Pida's. I heard the young Indian say: "It is my father's will."

"I'll never betray it," Sam replied.

"You will suffer ten times more torture then."

"Don't be absurd. Sam Hawkins tortured! Your father wanted to torture me before, at Rio Pecos, among the Apaches. Can you tell me what was the result?"

"The cur, Old Shatterhand, made him a cripple. But you are bound hand and foot, and well guarded; how can you escape from here?"

"That is my affair, dear little boy. Wait. You can't keep me."

"You shall be free if you will tell us where he was going."

"But I never will. The good Santer was so kind as to tell me, in order to frighten me, that you had ridden to Nugget Mountain to capture Winnetou and Old Shatterhand. That would make a stone laugh. Capture Old Shatterhand, my pupil -- ha! ha! ha! And now that you've failed you want me to tell you where they've gone. You think I must know, and I tell you frankly I do know, but you'll find out soon enough without my telling you, for --"

He was interrupted by a loud cry. I could not understand the words, but the tone was as though they were shouting: "Catch him, catch him," and I heard Winnetou's name echoed.

"Do you hear?" cried Sam in ecstasy. "Where Winnetou is, Old Shatterhand is also. They've come, they've come!"

The tumult in the village increased; I heard the Indians running. They had seen Winnetou, but he had got away. I saw the chief's son spring into his canoe, and heard him call to the sentinels: "Take your guns, and shoot the prisoner if any one tries to free him."

Then he paddled toward the shore.

I had intended to free Sam at once, but even if I had dared attempt it, armed as I was only with a knife, Pida's order put all thought of doing so out of the question. But an idea came to me. Pida was the chief's best beloved son. If I could get him in my hands I could demand Sam as ransom. The plan was a wild one, but it might succeed. A glance showed that the situation was favorable to the attempt. Winnetou had fled toward the Red River on the left, misleading his pursuers, for our camp lay toward the right. The cries of the Indians arose from that direction, to which the eyes of the sentinels also were turned, as they stood with their backs to me. Soon they crossed over to the other side where they could see better. The chief's son had reached the shore with his canoe, and was about to tie it. He stooped over, I crept up behind him; a blow knocked him down. I threw him into the canoe, sprang in myself, and paddled as hard as I could against the stream.

The rash stroke had succeeded! No one in the village had seen me, and Sam's guards were still staring in the opposite direction. I used all my strength to get out of the range of the village, lest the firelight should fall on me and betray me. I paddled to the right shore of the Salt Fork, laid the unconscious Pida in the grass, cut the rope from the canoe to bind him, gave it a push that sent it down the stream where it would not witness against me, took my prisoner on my shoulder, and started back to our camp. It was not an easy task, for not only was my burden heavy, but as Pida came to himself he struggled as much as he could to get away.

"Who are you?" he asked at last in a towering rage. "A miserable pale-face whom Tangua, my father, will catch in the morning and kill."

"Your father won't catch me; he can't walk," I answered.

"He has countless warriors whom he will send after me."

"I laugh at your warriors. It will be with them as it was with your father if they dare fight me."

"Ugh! Have you fought my father?"

"Yes, and he fell when my shot went through both his knees."

"Ugh, Ugh! So you are Old Shatterhand?" he asked, surprised.

"Who but Winnetou and Old Shatterhand would dare rush into your village and carry off the chief's son?"

"Ugh! Then I shall die, but you will not hear a moan of pain from my lips."

"We will not kill you; we are not murderers, like the Kiowas. If your father will give up the two palefaces he has with him, you shall be free."

"Hawkins and Santer?"

"Yes."

"He will give them up. His son is more precious to him than ten times ten Hawkins, and he has no respect for Santer."

After this Pida made no more resistance. I came at last opposite our island, and dawn was breaking, but the mist was too thick to allow me to see. "Hallo!" I cried.

"Hallo!" answered Winnetou's voice. "Is that my brother Shatterhand?"

"Yes."

"Then come; why do you call? It is dangerous."

"I have a prisoner; send over a good swimmer and a thong."

"I will come myself."

In a few' moments I saw his head in the water, and was thankful to see it, and know that he was safe. When he came over to me, and saw my prisoner, he said in amazement: "Ugh! Pida, the chief's son. Where did my brother capture him?"

"On the river shore, near Hawkins' island. I should have spoken to Sam and freed him, only you were discovered, so I had to be off."

"It was an unlucky chance. I had reached Santer's tent, when a Kiowa came over to speak to him. As they were talking the Indian saw me, and started toward me. I slipped away, but the firelight fell on me and the Kiowa recognized me. I went up, instead of down stream to deceive them, swam over and came here. And I have not got Santer."

"You shall get him. This young warrior shall be exchanged for him and Hawkins, and both he and I are sure the chief will agree to this."

"Ugh! That is good, very good. My brother has acted most wisely in securing Pida. It was the best thing that could have happened."

We tied our prize between us with his arms fast, but his legs left free to swim, and he was so far from resisting us that he willingly helped us as we crossed. The mist lay so thick over the river that we could not see twenty feet before us, but such a fog heightens every sound. We were not far from the shore when Winnetou said: "Hark! I heard something."

"What?"

"A sound like a paddle above us."

"Then let us wait."

We made such slight movements as were necessary to keep us above water, and listened. Yes; Winnetou was right; somebody was paddling down the river. Should we let him see us? It might be a spy, but it might be something else. It was most important to us to see what it was. I looked inquiringly at Winnetou. He understood, and said at once: "I will not go back. I must know who this is."

We lay still, hoping not to be seen. Pida could have betrayed us by a cry, but he did not, for he knew that in any case he was safe.

Now the splash of the paddle was close on us, and an Indian canoe cleft the fog. In it sat who? As Winnetou saw the man he uttered a great cry: "Santer, escaping!" my friend, usually so calm, was beside himself at the sight of his foe. He tried to free himself to swim to the canoe, but was so fast bound to Pida that he could not get away.

"I must be free. Help me; I must have him," he cried, drawing his knife and cutting the thongs.

Santer had heard Winnetou's exclamation; he looked over and saw us. "You --" he began, but stopped, took in our situation, threw the paddle in the canoe, snatched his gun, and cried: "Your last swim, you curs."

Fortunately Winnetou had cut himself free from Pida at that very moment; he darted forward as Pida and I dodged the shot, which fell harmless in the water.

Winnetou did not swim; he darted forward. He had his knife in his teeth, and flew after his enemy with long springs. I could only think of the stones I used to "skip" a cross the pond when I was a boy.

Santer was ready for another shot, and cried scornfully: "Come on, you cursed redskin. I'll send you after your father."

But he did not know Winnetou. The latter dove suddenly, intending to come up under the canoe and upset it. If he did this Santer's gun would be no more use to him, and there would be a struggle in which the Apache would be victor. Santer saw this, laid aside his gun quickly, and seized his paddle again. It was time he did, for Winnetou came up just where the canoe had been a moment before. Santer exerted himself, and got out of the reach of his furious enemy, crying: "Have you got me, dog? I'll keep my shot for our next meeting."

Winnetou used all his skill, but no swimmer, if he were the world's champion, could catch a canoe paddled down the stream. I called one of the Apaches whom the cries and the shot had brought to the shore, to help me bring Pida over, and Winnetou almost immediately returned. I had never seen him so excited. He said to his people: "Let my brothers get ready quickly. Santer has gone down the stream in a canoe, and we must go after him."

"Yes, we must go this instant," I agreed. "But what shall we do with Sam Hawkins and our two prisoners?"

"They will be left to you," replied Winnetou.

"Shall I stay here?"

"Yes. I must have the murderer of my father and sister, but your duty is to free Sam Hawkins. We must part."

"For how long?"

He considered a moment, and then said: "I do not know. The wishes and will of man depend on the Great Spirit. I thought I should be longer with my brother Shatterhand, but Manitou has denied this; He wills it otherwise."

"I wish that I could go with you to capture Santer, but I suppose I must save Sam; I can't forsake him."

"I would never wish you to do anything contrary to your duty; you must not. But if the Great Spirit wills, we shall meet again one day."

"Where?"

"When you ride from here go to the Bayou Pierre, and where the Pierre flows into this river you will find one of my warriors in case we can meet."

"And if I see no warrior?"

"Then I shall still be pursuing Santer, not knowing whither he has gone, and cannot tell you where to meet me. In that case ride with your three comrades to St. Louis, to the pale-faces who would build the road for the fire-steed. But I pray you come back to us as soon as the good Manitou allows it. You will ever be welcome in the pueblo of Rio Pecos, and if I am not there, you will learn where to find me."

While he was speaking the horses had been made ready. He gave his hand to Dick Stone and Will Parker in farewell, and then turned to me, saying: "My brother knows how glad our hearts were when we began our ride from Rio Pecos. Intschu-Tschuna and Nscho-Tschi were with us. When you return you will not hear the voice of the fairest of the daughters of the Apaches, who, instead of going to the States of the palefaces, has gone to the land of the departed. Justice now calls me from you, but love will bring you back to us. Will you promise to come back to us soon, my dear, dear brother Jack?""

I promise you. My heart goes with you, my dear brother Winnetou."

"Then may the good Manitou guide all your steps and protect you in all your ways. How!"

He put his arms around me and kissed me, gave a brief command to his people, mounted his horse and was gone. I looked after him till he had disappeared in the mist; it seemed to me I had lost a part of my very self.

It was night before I dared attempt the final stroke of our venturesome game. Then I crept alone in the darkness to the village, as Winnetou and I had done together the day before. Again I saw the fire burning, before which sat Tangua, with only his two younger sons now. His head was sunk, and he stared gloomily in the fire. Suddenly he began the deep, monotonous death chant; he was mourning the loss of his eldest, best-beloved son. Indian fashion I crawled around to the other side of the tent, rose up, and stood in full view before the chief.

"Why does Tangua sing the lamentation?" I asked.

"A brave warrior should not wail; wailing is for old squaws."

I could not describe how amazed he was. He tried to speak, but could not utter a word. He stared at me with bulging eyes, and at last stammered: "Old--Old--Shat--Shat--Shatter-- How came you here?"

"I have come to speak to you," I replied.

"Old Shatterhand," I heard echoing from side to side beyond the tent, and the two boys ran away.

The chief rallied, his face took on an expression of rage, and he called out a command of which I could understand nothing but my name, because he spoke in the Kiowa tongue. A moment later a howl of rage rang through the entire village; it seemed to me the earth shook beneath my feet, as all the warriors who had not gone on Winnetou's trail, which had long before been discovered, rushed into the tent with drawn knives. I drew my knife and cried in Tangua's ear: "Shall Pida be killed? He sent me to you."

He heard, in spite of the howling of his people, and raised his hand. Silence followed, though the Kiowas pressed threateningly around us. If looks of hatred could kill, I should have fallen dead. I sat down by Tangua, looked quietly in his face, blank with amazement at my boldness, and said: "There is enmity between me and Tangua; I am not to blame for it, nor do I object. He can see whether I fear him, since I am come here to speak to him. We will be brief. Pida is in our hands, and will be hanged to a tree if I am not back at an appointed time."

No word, no movement betrayed the effect of my words. The eyes of the chief flashed with rage that he could not harm me without endangering his son. He growled between his teeth: "How did he get in your power?"

"I was over there by the island last night when he spoke to Sam Hawkins, and I captured him."

"Ugh! Old Shatterhand is beloved by the wicked spirit, who protects him. Where is my son?"

"In a safe place, where you will not find him; he himself shall tell you where it is later. You can see from these words that I do not intend to kill him. We have another Kiowa prisoner; he and your son shall be free if you will give Sam Hawkins for them."

"Ugh! You shall have him. Bring back Pida and the other Kiowa brave."

"Bring them? Well, hardly. I know Tangua, and know that I can't trust him. I give you two for one, and am unusually good and generous to you. So give me Hawkins, and send four braves with me to bring back Pida and the other prisoner. In the meantime I must see Sam, and learn from his own mouth how he has been treated."

"I must first consult my oldest braves. Go to the next tent and wait."

"Very well; only make it short, for if I'm not back at a certain time Pida will be hanged."

To an Indian hanging is the most shameful of deaths, so one may fancy how Tangua liked this remark. Nevertheless, he sent a brave to bring Sam to the tent where I waited. The little man sprang to me, holding out his fettered hands, and crying jubilantly: "Hello, Old Shatterhand. I knew you'd come. Do you want your old Sam back?"

"Yes," I said, "and the tenderfoot has come to tell you are the greatest master of the art of spying. Have they treated you badly?"

"Badly? What is the matter with you? Every Kiowa has loved me like his own baby."

"That's lucky for them now. The council seems to be over."

I went back to Tangua, and found him ready, under the pressure of circumstances, to agree to my proposition. Two canoes were made ready, and four armed braves accompanied Sam and me to bring back the hostages. The Indians were enraged at being obliged to let me go with their prisoner, and Tangua said to me in parting: "When I have my son back, I will send the whole tribe after you. We will find your trail, and catch you, even if you ride through the air."

I did not think it necessary to reply to this threat, and we departed down the river, a howl following us till we were too far away to hear it. We gave up our prisoners, who left us without a word of farewell.

Sam threw up his arms as they were unbound, crying: "Free, free again. It will be a long day before I forget you, Jack Hildreth."

We waited till we could no longer hear the splash of the paddles of the returning canoes, and then mounted, and rode down stream, away from the unattractive neighborhood of the Kiowa village.

CHAPTER VI

THE LAKE OF BURNING OIL

IT was a long journey to the meeting-place which Winnetou had appointed, and when it was accomplished, after many weary days and nights, the hope of finding the chief at its end was not realized. But he had been able to send us a message about himself and his mission by an Apache scout, and that was some comfort.

Thus far Santer had eluded Winnetou successfully. The scoundrel had murdered the two traders whom we had met on our way to the Kiowa village, had taken their goods, and was now on his way to the northwest trading. Winnetou was sure that sooner or later he would fall into his hands. This was the message I received from him, with a reminder of my promise to return to him soon, and with it came a present of a horse that would have made Pegasus preen his wings in jealous fear of being considered an inferior animal. He was called Swallow, so fleet was he, and during the long ride through Louisiana to the point where I took the boat for St. Louis, we learned to know and love each other. Sam, Dick and Will left me here, returning to the prairie and the wild life which was their choice, and I went on alone.

I stayed in St. Louis only long enough to turn over my measurements for the railroad, and to fit myself out with some much needed clothing, and a new Henry rifle, and then Swallow and I started again for the West in search of new adventures, and to rejoin our Apache friend. I was to meet him not far from a town called New Venango in the Wyoming oil region. I had ridden all day, and both Swallow and his master were tired, and longed for the first glimpse of the little town where we were to rest for the night, when the horse raised his drooping head suddenly, and sniffed the air in a way that showed that strangers were near by. He was right. At some distance from us I saw two figures, one a man's, the other that of a boy of about fourteen, dressed in full trapper regalia; both were mounted.

As I came up with them the lad waved his riding whip, and cried in a fresh, cheery young treble: "Good day, sir. What were you looking for so hard just now?"

"For a town, my bold trapper, and it's harder to find than prairie dogs."

"That's because the only one about here is over behind that bluff."

"The only prairie dog?"

"No; the only town. It's New Venango. Is that the one you're looking for?"

"Yes."

"Then come along with us. This is the man I'm staying with. His name's Foster, and he keeps the store and hotel at New Venango."

"The store; then New Venango can't be crowded with business blocks."

"It's got enough," returned the youngster, with touchy pride in the youthful city. "New Venango is going to be the biggest city in the West some day."

"I've no doubt. There are more embryo 'biggest cities' in the West than there are Washington headquarters houses in the East. However, I'll be glad to go with you to this one, and rest under your friend's hospitable roof."

Foster growled out some inarticulate reply; he struck me as a villainous-looking piece of humanity, but I liked the boy at once, though anything more patronizing and self-possessed than his manner would be hard to imagine.

"That isn't a bad horse you've got there," he said, looking at Swallow with the eye of a judge of horse flesh. "Is he for sale?"

"Not at any price. He has taken me through many dangers, and I owe him my life more than once."

"He has had Indian training," he said next, to my surprise. "Where did you get him?"

"From a friend of mine, Winnetou, the Apache chief."

He looked at me in surprise. "He's the greatest Indian in the world. You don't look --" he stopped.

"Well?" I prompted.

"Oh, I don't know; I thought you were a surveyor, or naturalist, or something like that. Are you Winnetou's friend, honest?"

"Honest Injun," I said laughing.

"You've good shooting irons too," continued my critical comrade. "What do you think of this pistol?"

He drew out of his saddle pocket a rusty old affair, and holding it up triumphantly said: "It dates from Anno Pocahontas, but it's all right."

He dropped behind me, and in a moment I felt a jar of my hat, and saw the sunflower I had picked from the golden carpet of the prairie and stuck in my hat-band fall shattered at Swallow's feet.

"Not so bad," I said coolly, inwardly wondering what to think of the interesting youngster. I looked at him as he rode half a horse's length ahead of me, and the setting sun bathed him in its golden light. He was 'brown and beautiful' as the Holy Writ tells us the young David was, and his peculiar features had an expression of strength, in spite of their youthful softness, while every movement spoke of self-reliance and determination which prevented me treating him as a child.

"Are you an American?" I asked at last.

"More American than you are, for my mother was an Indian of the tribe of the Mascalero-Apaches."

This explained the sharp-cut features, and the depth of his coloring. He said his mother was dead, but that his father still lived. I dared ask no more questions, though they were not prompted by mere curiosity. I wanted very much to know more about the mother, who was of the same tribe as Winnetou -- my tribe by adoption.

"Do you see that smoke that looks as though it came out of the ground?" the boy asked, pointing ahead with his whip.

"Ah, then we are at the bluff at last, and that is New Venango in the hollow?" I said. "Neither Swallow nor I am sorry."

We paused a moment to look down at the valley, encircled by rocks, in the midst of which flowed a little stream, seeking its outlet through the stone. All the ground before us seemed to be covered with contrivances for drawing out the oil; close to the stream stood a drill in full blast, mid-way in the valley was a refinery, and all about were tubs, casks and tanks for the crude oil.

"Yes, that is the bluff," said Harry, as his silent companion had once called the boy. "Over yonder is the store, restaurant, hotel and everything in one, and this is the way down; it's rather steep. We'll have to dismount."

I did so, and Harry added: "Get your horse by the bridle; you must lead him."

"Swallow will come of his own accord," I replied, and we descended to the valley, remounted, and rode to the hotel, restaurant, store, notary's and justice's office, undertaker's, carpenter's, to all of which one and the same door admitted.

As we dismounted, this "concentrated inhabitant," as Mark Twain called a similar worthy, took Swallow by the bridle. "I want to buy this horse," he said. "How much do you want for him?"

"He's not for sale."

"I'll give you two hundred."

I laughed, and shook my head.

"Three hundred."

"Don't bother about price, sir. He's not for sale," I repeated.

"Three hundred, and whatever you want out of the store."

"Do you really think I'd sell that horse unless I were forced to?"

"I'll throw in mine. I must have him; I like him."

"I believe that, but you can't have him; you're too poor to buy him."

"Too poor!" he gave me a contemptuous look. "I own half these oil wells. I am able to buy thus and such horses."

"Maybe you could buy a thousand, but you can't buy this one. If you want a horse, go to a dealer, but take your hand off mine."

"Look here! You're tramping round the country; you ought to be glad to get money honestly."

"Keep a civil tongue in your head. If you had to deal with most Westerners you'd be paid in powder and shot for that remark."

"I'd have you understand, young man, that you can't come do any of your prairie business here. I am the law in New Venango, and if any one doesn't do as I wish willingly, he does it anyhow. Now shall I have the horse or not?"

"No," I answered. "Take your hand away."

I reached out for the bridle, he pushed me back, and swung himself into the saddle." I'll show you whether I'll buy a horse or not if I take the notion. There is mine; you may have him. Take what you want out of the store, and you shall have your money when you want it. Come, Harry."

He rode on Swallow around the house, and out of sight.

Harry loitered a moment to ask: "Do you know what a coyote is?"

"Yes," I replied. "He's a frightened beast that runs when a dog barks."

"Well, you're a coyote." with an indescribable, contemptuous wave of the hand he followed the "law" of New Venango.

I took it calmly, for I knew my plans, and that I had not lost Swallow. I went into the hotel, not the store; that is, I turned to the right instead of to the left in the narrow passage, and ate a hearty supper, albeit the cook could hardly have served as chef at Delmonico's.

When the evening was well advanced, and darkness had fallen over the valley, I went out to look up Swallow. I knew no stranger could unsaddle him, and put him in a stall, so I felt pretty sure I should find him supping out of doors. I had learned that Foster lived about a quarter of a mile from his concentrated place of business. My way was along the river, and I noticed something that I had been too much occupied with my young companion to see when I arrived, and this was that the oil smoke which filled the entire valley, was thicker by the river. The stream must carry with it then a considerable quantity of crude oil. There was a light on the verandah of the rambling building which was Foster's house, and I concluded that he was enjoying his evening pipe in the pleasant warmth of the late spring evening. I came up quietly in the shadow. As I reached the fence that enclosed the place

I heard a soft sniffing of the air, and I knew that Swallow was in the yard, trying to make sure that his master was really coming.

I vaulted the fence in the friendly shadow of a tree, and heard Harry, who lay in a hammock, saying: "I think it's a queer scheme, Mr. Foster. It won't work, I believe."

"What do you know of such things? You are a boy. The price of oil is so low because the market is glutted. If we keep back our oil for a month it will bring up prices. I'll let it flow into the river till the price rises, then I'll set things going again, send my tanks East, and make a hundred thousand easy."

"Well, it doesn't seem square to me," remarked Harry. "And I wouldn't do it."

Foster was about to explain his plans further, evidently more to satisfy himself than to inform the boy, when there came a thundering crash as though the earth had burst under us. The ground trembled, and as I turned in alarm; I saw in the lower part of the valley where the drill was still at work, a glowing stream of fire, fully fifty feet high, shoot up, sink to earth, and with the utmost rapidity overflow the low land. At the same moment a thick, greasy smoke filled the air, and the atmosphere seamed charged with fire.

I recognized the phenomenon, for I had seen it in all its terror in the Kanawha valley, and I sprang out before the horror-stricken people who had rushed from every door.

"Put out the lights," I shouted. "Quick, put out the lights. The drill has struck oil, and you have neglected to forbid lights near it. The gas is escaping, and has ignited. Put out the lights, or in two minutes the whole valley will burn."

I sprang into the house to turn off the different gadgets, but a lamp burned in an inner room, and I saw lights glimmering down by the store. The spurting oil which had spread with incredible speed over the whole valley had reached the river now, and there was only question of escaping with life.

"Save yourselves!" I cried. "Fly, fly, in heaven's name. Try for the-hills."

Without waiting to see the fate of any one I snatched Harry up, and the next moment was in the saddle with him in my arms. Harry, misunderstanding my action, and not knowing the extent of the danger, resisted me with all his might, but in such a moment a man possesses strength beyond nature, and Harry's struggles died out in the grasp with which I held him. Swallow, whose instinct made the guidance of bit and the urging of spur superfluous, bore us away like the wind. We could not get to the mountain path by which we had entered New Venango, for it was submerged in the fiery stream. We could only find deliverance down the river, but I had not seen anything like a street in that direction, and thought, on the contrary, that the cliffs were so close together that only the river could get through them.

"Is there any way out?" I cried in anguish.

"No, no," Harry gasped, with convulsive efforts to get away. "Let me go, I tell you, let me go. I don't need your help. I can take care of myself."

Of course I paid no attention to this, but scanned the horizon for a way out. I felt a prick in my throat, and the boy cried: "What do you want with me? Let me go, or I'll stick your own knife in you." I saw a blade flash in his hand; he had drawn my knife. I had no time for a long contest; I caught both his wrists in my right hand, while I held him fast with my left arm.

The danger increased with each second. The burning stream had reached the refineries, and the tanks burst with a cannon-like explosion, and poured their contents into the sea of fire, increasing it, and making it flow faster every instant. The atmosphere was hot to suffocation; I felt as though I were boiling in a tank of seething water, and scorched inside. I almost lost consciousness, but not quite, for not only was my life at stake, but the boy's.

"Come, Swallow; come, good Swall--" the fearful heat burned my mouth; I could no longer speak. But it was not necessary; the brave, splendid beast rushed on with incredible speed. I saw one thing; there was no way out on this side the stream. So into the water, into the water, over to the other side. A light touch on the bridle, a spring of the obedient horse, and the waters closed over us. I felt new life, new strength pulsing through my veins, but Swallow had disappeared. Never mind; only over, over!

Swallow had been faster than the fire, but now it came, flaming as high as the black heavens, leaping down the river, and finding ever new food in the petroleum on its waters. In a moment, in a second, it must reach me. The now unconscious boy hung to me with a death-like grasp. I swam as never before, or rather I did not swim, I leaped through the seething water. I felt frightful pain, so frightful that I wondered whether it was death. Then came a hot breath at my side. Swallow, you blessed, you true horse, is it you? Here is the shore -- again in the saddle -- I cannot -- my marrow is withering away -- Lord, God help -- I can't lie here -- once more. Try! Ah! I am up! Swallow, go on, go -- where you like, only away, away from this lake of hell. We were going, I knew only that; where I did not ask. My eyes lay like melted iron in their sockets, and the light was burning my brain; my tongue hung from between my dry lips, my body felt as though it were a burning tinder, whose ashes might at any moment fall apart. The horse under me panted and groaned with almost human agony; he leaped, he jumped; he shot over crags, clefts, ledges, peaks with feline, sinuous motions. I had clasped his neck with my right arm, while the left still held the boy fast. One more spring, one long, frightful spring -- at last, at last the precipice is crossed, a few feet further and we were in the prairie, and Swallow stood still.

I sank to the ground, overcome by the reaction from the long strain of nerve and muscle. I raised myself slowly, threw both arms around the neck of the faithful, incomparable beast, who was trembling in every limb, and kissed him with convulsive sobs, and a fervor beyond words. "Thank you, Swallow; my blessed, blessed Swallow. You have saved me; you have saved us both. I'll never forget this hour."

The heavens glowed blood red, and the vapors from the freed elements hung in thick black masses, streaked with purple, over the ruined hearths. But I had no time to look at this, for Harry lay before me, white, cold, and stiff, the knife still clasped in his hand. I thought him dead, that he had drowned in the river when I would rescue him from the flames. His clothing was wet, and clung to his lifeless limbs, and the sullen reflection of the flames beyond the edge of the plain played on his blanched face. I took him in my arms, pushed back his hair from his forehead, rubbed his temples, put my lips to his mouth to breathe life into his motionless chest; in short, did all that in my own condition I could do to call him back to life. At last a quiver passed over his body, and I felt the beating of his heart, the flutter of returning breath. He opened his eyes wide, and stared about with an expression of fear and wonder. Then his gaze became conscious, and he started up with a loud cry. "Where am I? W ho are you? What has happened?"

"You are saved from the flames below us."

With the sound of my voice, and the flash of a flame darting higher than the others, full consciousness returned to him.

"Saved? Flames? Oh, good heavens, is it true the valley is burned?" he raised his arm threateningly. "You're a coward," he said. "A mean coward, a coyote, as I told you before. You could have saved them all, but you ran like a sneaking cur. I despise you. I must go back to them."

He started away; I took his hand to detain him. "Stay here," I said. "There is nothing more to be done for them."

"Let me alone. I won't stay with a coward." he snatched his hand away, and ran off. I felt something between my fingers. It was a ring which he had pulled off as he broke away. I followed him, but he was soon lost in the shadow of the cliffs.

I could not be angry with the boy; he was only a boy still, and the tragedy had so horrified him that he could not judge fairly. I slipped the ring on my little finger, and went back to take the rest I so sorely needed. And my nerves still quivered, and the valley in which the petroleum was yet burning seemed to me like the infernal regions from which I had escaped. Swallow lay close to me; there was grass around us, but he did not eat; the brave beast was as overcome as I was, or even more so.

What had become of the inhabitants of the valley? The question kept me awake; I longed to forget for a moment the horrors of that night, but sleep would not come. So I watched till morning, and all night long the awful fire leaped in a fountain of flame toward heaven, and so it would burn while the oil still came up through the opening the drill had made.

Daylight modified the intensity of the glow, but as the sun came up I saw that with the exception of one little house on the side of the hill where the fire could not reach, everything had been destroyed. Before the solitary little building that had escaped destruction, stood some men, and I saw that Harry was with them. The venturesome boy had dared go back during the night. It was easy enough to go now by daylight, but the risk he had taken then, exhausted as he was too, was frightful to think of.

The path by which I had come the day before had reappeared, and I rose to follow it. I saw Harry pointing to me, and one of the men went into the house, and returned in a moment with a gun. He came to the river bank to await me, and when I had got within speaking distance called out: "Hallo you! What are you doing here? Get out, if you don't want a bullet between your ribs."

"I came to see if I could help you," I answered.

"I know," he sneered. "A man appreciates such help as yours."

"Besides, I want to speak to the boy Harry," I added. "I have something to give him."

"Oh, get out with you! We know what such a fellow as you would give him. First you're cowardly and hard-hearted, and then you set fire to the oil out of revenge."

For a moment I could not speak. He must have taken my silence as a sign of a guilty conscience, for he continued: "So! How surprised you are! Yes, we know mighty well what you are. If you don't get out this minute you'll never be able to go."

He pointed his gun at me, but I found my tongue, and cried angrily: "Are you crazy, man? There is no question of the oil being set afire. It was ignited by your own lamps; the horrible accident was the result of your own carelessness."

"I know, I know. Will you go, or shall I shoot?" he said.

"Would I have saved the boy at the risk of my life if I had been such a villain?" I asked.

"Humbug! If you had not run away, and had so chosen, you could have saved everybody, and now they are all burned -- dead. Here's your pay." he fired at me as he spoke.

I was too indignant to move; I stood perfectly still, which was fortunate, for his aim was bad, and I escaped. Instinctively my finger sought my trigger for a return shot, but of course I did not pull it. I turned around, slowly ascending the path without looking back. If instead of receiving gratitude for saving Harry I was to be treated like a criminal, there was nothing left to do but shake the dust of what had been New Venango from my feet. Once more I mounted Swallow, and rode away from a scene which has ever been to me like a horrible nightmare.

CHAPTER VII

THE ATTACK ON THE TRAIN

I WAS glad to turn my thoughts from the horrors I had just passed through, and the unpleasant ending of my brief acquaintance with Harry, to the fact that I was riding to meet Winnetou again. Our meeting place was only a day's ride from New Venango, but I had to wait there a whole week for Winnetou. At last he came, and I did not realize myself, impatient as I was for his coming, how glad I should be to see him, till I spied his lithe, straight figure on the horizon, and heard the cry with which he spurred his horse to meet me.

"My dear, dear brother Jack," he said with more emotion than I had thought one of his race could show, as he sprang from his horse, and laid his arms over my shoulders, looking eagerly into my eyes. "You have come to keep your promise. My heart rejoices like the morning when the night is past, and the sun appears."

"And I am as glad as the earth is glad when winter is over, and she feels the touch of spring," I said, taking both his hands, and pressing them joyfully. "Honestly, Winnetou, I knew I wanted to see you, but I did not realize how glad I'd be."

He caught his breath in a little laugh of pure happiness.

"Have you any trace of Santer?"

His face clouded. "He is everywhere; I have followed him in vain since I parted from my brother. Now I have heard he is near here. But his fever for gold will bring him to Nugget Mountain; at last he will fall into my hands. I will take my brother to the dwelling place of Old Firehand, who is my good friend, and a renowned trapper and warrior."

I was very glad to learn this, for I had heard a great deal of this famous man, and was delighted at the prospect of seeing him.

We rode till the shadows were lengthening, and evening was beginning to close in, when we paused on an elevation which swelled up in the prairie like a wave in the midst of the ocean. I took out my field glass to look over the stretch of prairie thus brought into view, and had scarcely adjusted it when I saw a long, straight line stretching to the furthest western point the eye could see. I gave the glass to Winnetou, who looked through it with an admiring and wondering "Ugh."

"Does my brother know what that long trail is?" I asked. "It is not the buffaloes', nor was it made by the feet of the red men."

"Yes, I know. It is the path of the fire-steed which we are looking at." he raised the glass again, and looked with great interest through this new device for lessening distance. Suddenly he lowered it, sprang from his horse, and hastily got behind the mound. Of course he had some good reason for doing so, and I imitated his action without asking why. "There are Indians over there by the fire-steed's path," he exclaimed. "They are hidden, but I saw their horses."

He was wise to withdraw from our observation post so quickly, for we should certainly have been seen. "What does my brother think is the design of these people?" I asked.

"They want to destroy the path of the fire-steed," Winnetou replied.

"That is what I think. Let me watch them." taking the glass from Winnetou I crept carefully forward. Although I was sure they had no suspicion that we were near I kept under cover as far as possible, and got far enough toward them to count them as I lay on the ground. There were thirty, decked with war-paint, and armed with arrows as well as fire-arms. They had several extra horses, and from this I was sure they were after booty. I heard some one breathing softly behind me. Drawing my knife, I turned around: it was Winnetou "Ugh!" he exclaimed "My brother is very bold to come so far. They are Poncas, the most daring of the Sioux, and there is Paranoh, their white chief."

I looked at him in surprise. "Their white chief?" I echoed.

"Has my friend never heard of Paranoh, the fierce chief of Atabaskah? No one knows whence he came, but he is a mighty warrior, and was adopted by the red men in a council of the tribes. As the gray-haired men went to Manitou, he received the calumet of chieftainship, and has taken many scalps. Then he was beguiled by the wicked spirit, and treated his braves like slaves, and was cast out. Now he dwells in the councils of the Poncas, and will lead them to do great deeds. Winnetou has measured tomahawks with him, but this white man is full of knavery; he does not fight honorably."

"I see that he is a traitor. He will stop the fire-steed, and kill, and rob my brethren."

"The white men?" asked Winnetou, astonished. "He is of the same color. What will my brother do?"

"I will wait to see whether Paranoh destroys the fire-steed's path, and if he does I will ride to meet my brethren, and warn them."

The darkness grew deeper every moment, and made it more difficult to keep our eye on the enemy. As it was necessary to know exactly what the Indians were doing, I asked Winnetou to go back to the horses, and await me there while I spied on them. He agreed to this, but added: "If my brother is in danger let him imitate the cry of the prairie chicken, and I will come to his assistance." he went back and I crawled, lying flat on the ground, in the direction of the railroad, listening intently to every sound. It was a long time before I reached it, but at last I did get there, and with redoubled caution crawled to the other side of the place where I had seen the Poncas. When I was near them I could see that they were busy about something. There were large rocks all around this place, an unusual thing in the prairie, and that was the reason they selected it for carrying out their design. I heard them piling on the track rocks which must be very large and heavy, judging from the way the Indians puffed. There was not a moment to lose, and after I had crawled back for a short distance, I sprang up, and ran as fast as I could to where I had left Winnetou.

We laid our plans hastily, mounted, and went in a rapid trot along the track toward the east. A little moonlight would have been most acceptable, but the clear shimmer of the stars was enough to show us our way. A half an hour passed, and then another; there was no longer any danger for the approaching train if we could only succeed in attracting the engineer's attention. We let our horses walk, and rode on in silence.

At last we decided the time had come. We both dismounted, and fastened our horses securely. We gathered the dry grass into a heap, and twisting it into a sort of torch, peppered it with powder, and calmly waited events, listening intently in the darkness, and keeping our eyes in the direction where the train should appear.

At last, after what seemed a little eternity of waiting, the light glimmered far, far away, tiny at first, but gradually growing larger. Then we heard the rumble; the moment had come. I drew my revolver and fired into the bundle of dried grass, which quickly ignited. Swinging this improvised torch with one arm, I held up the other as a signal to stop. The engineer saw me, for the instant the torch was raised he whistled "down brakes," and the car wheels groaned, slackened, stood still.

Giving Winnetou a sign to follow me I ran before the locomotive, and holding up my coat which I had taken off for this purpose, before the headlight, I shouted: "Put out your lights."

Instantly the light was gone. The men on the Far Western roads have presence of mind, and are quick in action. Having obeyed my suggestion, the engineer called out from his cab: "Why are you covering our reflector, man? I hope there's nothing wrong beyond?"

"We must be in darkness," I replied. "There are Indians up above who are waiting to wreck the train."

"You don't say! If that is so you're the bravest fellow that ever blessed this cursed region." and jumping out, he wrung my hand till it ached.

In a moment we were surrounded by the passengers: "What is it? What's up? Why are we stopping?" echoed on every side. In a few words the situation was explained.

"We aren't many, passengers and all," said the engineer, "but we are well armed. Do you know how many Indians there are?"

"I counted thirty."

"Good! We'll do them up. But who's that man over there? By George! An Indian!" he drew and aimed at Winnetou, who had followed me, and stood half in shadow behind me.

"Hold on!" I cried. "He's my companion; he'd be glad to know the bold rider of the fire-steed."

"Oh, that's another thing. Call him over. What's his name?"

"He is Winnetou, the Apache chief."

"Winnetou!" he exclaimed loudly, and as he did so a man pushed forward through the group of passengers. "Is Winnetou here?" he asked.

He was a powerfully built man dressed like a trapper, and his tone was loud and cheery. He went over to Winnetou, and said with a ring of pleasure in his big voice: "Has Winnetou forgotten his friend's face and voice?"

"Ugh!" exclaimed Winnetou with equal pleasure. "How can Winnetou forget Old Firehand, the greatest of the white hunters, though he has not seen him for many moons?"

"Old Firehand, Old Firehand," rose on all sides, while every one crowded around to see the most renowned of the Indian fighters, to whom rumor attributed deeds of almost incredible daring.

"Old Firehand?" ejaculated the engineer. "Why didn't you tell me who you were, man? I'd have seen you had the state-room."

"Thank you, I was all right. But we mustn't waste precious time. We must decide what we're going to do about these Indians. And are you Winnetou's friend?" he asked turning to me. "Then you can count me another. Here's my hand."

"Yes, he is my friend," said Winnetou. "My friend and brother. We have drunk one another's blood in the bond of brotherhood."

"Is that so?" exclaimed Old Firehand quickly, coming nearer me, and looking at me closely. "Then you must be --"

"Old Shatterhand," said Winnetou, finishing his sentence for him. "Beneath whose hand every foe falls to the ground."

"Old Shatterhand, Old Shatterhand," everybody cried, pressing around me, as they had around Old Firehand.

"You are Old Shatterhand?" cried the engineer delighted. "Old Firehand, Old Shatterhand, and Winnetou. What a lucky meeting. With the three most famous, and most invincible men in the West we are sure to succeed, and all is up with the Indians. You tell us what to do, and we will obey you."

"They are thirty red villains," said Old Firehand, "and we'll shoot them in a heap."

"They are men," I remarked.

"Beasts in the shape of men," he answered sternly." I have heard enough of you to know you are forbearing with these fellows, but I am of a different way of thinking. I suppose you realize they'd have killed every man on this train? If you'd suffered what I have you'd look at things in a different light. And as to Paranoh, I have a reckoning with him which only blood can wipe out."

"How!" assented the usually quiet Winnetou. There must be some reason, I thought, for this strong feeling.

"You are quite right," said the engineer. "Forbearance in this case would be wrong. Tell us your plan."

"The train hands will stay with the cars. The passengers can come with us, if they like the adventure, and we'll teach these villains that it's not just the thing to wreck a train. We'll creep up to them in the darkness. As they have no idea we're near them the surprise will be as effectual as our weapons. As soon as we're through with them we'll signal with fire for the train to come on, only it must be slow, for we might not clear the track perfectly. Now, who will come?"

"I! I! I!" cried every voice.

"Then take your weapons, and come. We've no time to lose, for the Indians know the train is due, and if it doesn't show up they'll get suspicious."

We started, Winnetou and I ahead. The night was very still, and we had to be on the alert for the slightest rustle. The moon had arisen, and though it made it harder for us to conceal ourselves, it was an advantage in other ways. Occasionally we could see a figure appear on the horizon, over the mound where we had discovered the Poncas. They had stationed a sentinel there to watch for the train, but if he happened to turn his eye from the track he might easily discover us. After a few minutes we could see the others lying motionless on the ground. We moved up until we were directly over against the murderous band, and lay ready, with guns cocked. The first thing was to disable the sentinel, an undertaking that few but Winnetou could carry out. The man could see the smallest thing in the moonlight, and it was so still he could hear the slightest motion, and even if these difficulties were overcome, it would be necessary to spring on him, when the others would be certain to see the attack. Nevertheless Winnetou willingly undertook to solve this difficult problem. He slid forward, and in a few minutes the watch seemed to sink into the earth, yet the next instant was standing erect again, in his full stature. This movement had taken only a moment, brief as a flash of lightning, yet I knew that in it Winnetou had pulled the sentinel down by his feet as he stabbed him, and had risen himself in his place. The sentinel was no longer the Ponca, but Winnetou.

This was one of this marvelous Indian's feats, and through it our greatest difficulty was over. We were ready now to attack, but before the signal to advance could be given a shot rattled behind me. One of our band had been careless enough to keep his finger on his trigger, and the revolver had gone off. We could not delay now, and sprang out on our foe. The Indians rushed for their horses with horrible yells. "Shoot the horses," cried Old Firehand, "and then forward."

Our shots rattled; the horses fell, and there was before us a tangled mass of horses, their riders trying to crawl from under them.

Old Firehand and Winnetou had thrown themselves in the snarl brandishing their tomahawks, while I kept the Indians at bay by shooting at the horses whenever a rider tried to get through his fallen comrades. When I had used my last cartridge I laid aside my rifle, and gun, drew my tomahawk, and hastened to the side of Old Firehand and Winnetou. We three were the only ones who really fought the Poncas. I had strongly suspected the passengers from the train would not be much use, and it proved to be the case.

I spied Paranoh among the heap of Indians, and tried to get at him. Evading me, he got close to the Apache, tried to dodge again, but Winnetou sprang on him crying: "Paranoh! Will the Atabaskah dog fly before the chief of the Apaches? The earth's mouth shall drink his blood, and the vulture's claws shall tear his body, but his scalp shall hang at the belt of the Apache."

He threw away his tomahawk, drew his knife, and seized the white chief by the throat, but he was prevented from giving the fatal stroke. As he cast himself on the Ponca with this loud cry that was contrary to his custom, Old Firehand had glanced toward him, and seen his foe. In this rapid glance he had recognized the man he hated with all the bitterness of his Soul, and whom he had sought for seven years. "Tim Finnerty!" he cried, flinging aside the Indians like straw, and springing through them to Winnetou, whose hand, raised to strike, he seized. "Stop, brother; this man is mine."

Paranoh stood perfectly still as he heard his name called, but as soon as his eyes fell on Old Firehand he wrenched himself free from Winnetou's hand, and fled. Instantly I shook off the Indian with whom I had been fighting, and pursued him, for I knew he was Winnetou's deadly enemy, and the last moment had shown me Old Firehand had good cause to hate him. I heard Winnetou say: "Let Old Firehand stay here. My young white brother will catch and kill the Atabaskah crow. He has the foot of the storm, and no one can escape him."

These words naturally spurred me to do my best. I was gaining on the fugitive, the distance between us was lessening, I could hear his panting breath. I had no other weapon than the empty revolver, and my bowie knife, which I drew. I had dropped my tomahawk, for it would hinder me in running. Paranoh sprang aside to let me pass him in my haste, intending to come on me from behind. I saw through this maneuver, and turned just as he did, so that we should collide, and thus my knife ran into him up to the hilt. The collision was so violent that we both fell, but he did not rise as I picked myself up, and I did not know whether he was fatally wounded or not. But he did not move a limb; I could not see that he breathed, and I drew out my knife. It was not the first enemy I had laid low, but this was one of my own race, and I found myself hoping he was not dead, though he so richly deserved to die. As I stood looking at him I heard a quick breath behind me. I turned sharply, but had nothing to fear. It was Winnetou, who with loving unity had followed me, and now stood beside me.

"My brother is as quick as the arrow of the Apaches, and his knife goes true to its mark," he said as he looked at the form before us.

"Where is Old Firehand?" I asked.

"He is as strong as the bear in the time of the melting snow, but his foot is held by the hand of the years. Will not my brother take the scalp of the Atabaskah?"

"I leave that for my red friend," I replied. With three cuts the scalp lock was severed from the head of the dead man. How bitter must have been the hatred of the humane Winnetou for this Finnerty!

I had withdrawn a little during this proceeding, which I could not bear to look upon, and I saw some dark forms coming toward us.

"There are six Poncas who seem to be looking for some one. Winnetou must hide, for unarmed as we are it would be foolhardy to let them see us," I said.

The Apache crawled backward, close to the ground, and I followed. The Indians paused when they came to the scene of my meeting with Paranoh, and uttered an "Ugh" of surprise at seeing a body lying there. But when they came up to him, recognized him, and saw that he had been scalped, they uttered a howl of rage.

That was a critical moment for us. We were in instant danger of discovery, so we resolved on a bold stroke. Leaping out we were on the horses' backs in a trice (the horses from which the Poncas had just dismounted) and dashed away at a mad gallop. It was funny to think of the blank faces which must look on our sight as they realized the trick that had been played them, and even the grave Winnetou could not help a laughing "Ugh" as he pictured their dismay.

We were anxious about Old Firehand, who might also have met a band of the Indians. Nor was this anxiety lessened when on our return to our comrades we found that he had not come back, although we had been gone so long.

"My brother, Old Firehand, has lost Paranoh's trail," said Winnetou, "and may be attacked by his enemies. I will go with Old Shatterhand to look for him."

"Yes, we must go quickly," I agreed, "for he may be in danger."

We lighted the signal fire for the train to come on, shook hands cordially with the passengers, who were unspeakably grateful for their rescue, resumed the weapons we had cast away in following Paranoh, and hastened in the direction in which we had last seen Old Firehand.

At first the noise of the approaching train drowned all other sounds, but after we had gone far enough from this, the profound silence of the night enveloped us, and still nothing revealed to us the whereabouts of our missing comrade. After a long and fruitless search we were about to go back to the railroad, thinking he too must have returned by this time, when we heard a cry in the distance.

"That must be our brother, Old Firehand, for the Poncas would not betray themselves by a cry as they are fleeing," said Winnetou. "Quick, we must go to him; he is in danger."

We separated, Winnetou going east, I toward the north, whence I thought the sound had come. As I ran forward I found I was right, for the cry was repeated, much louder than before. And then I saw a group of men fighting. "I'm coming, Old Firehand; I'm coming," I shouted, running still faster.

Old Firehand was kneeling on the ground; he had sunk down wounded, and was defending himself against three foes, having already laid three others low. They were the same six Poncas whom we had seen, and whose horses we had taken. Each stroke might end Old Firehand, and I was fully fifty feet away. So I paused, and raised my revolver, which I had reloaded. The light of the moon was uncertain, my pulse was rapid, and my breath short from running, dangerous conditions under which to shoot, for I might hit him whom I wished to aid; however, I must venture it.

Three shots in rapid succession; the three foes fell. I ran up to Old Firehand, who cried: "Thank God! That was the nick of time, the very last moment."

"You are wounded; seriously?" I asked.

"Not to endanger my life. Tomahawk cuts in the legs, that's all. The fellows could not get at me from above, so they hacked away below. But what a shot you are! In such a light and after such a run to hit all three in the head! I had only my knife and my fist, for I had thrown away my other weapons. If you hadn't come up I'd be in eternity now. I won't forget this debt to Old Shatterhand."

Winnetou joined us at this moment, and we managed to get Old Firehand back to the horses. We found that we should be forced to wait at least a week before he would be able to ride, however, so we carried him half a day's journey to where there was water and woods, and waited his recovery in safety, and gratitude for the happy ending of our good night's work.

CHAPTER VIII

A CHAPTER OF SURPRIZES

SEVERAL days had passed, and Old Firehand had recovered sufficiently to ride with us to his "village." the night before we were to start I sat with him by the camp fire, and he opened the case hanging around his neck, took out the pipe he carried in it, filled it, and passed the tobacco pouch to me. As I filled my pipe, and returned the pouch to him the firelight fell on my little finger, and Harry's little ring showed bright in the flame. Old Firehand's sharp eyes caught the gleam of the gold, and with a surprised face he asked: "What is that ring you wear?"

"It is the memorial of a horrible hour in my life," I replied.

"Will you let me look at it?"

I did so. Scarcely had he taken it in his hand than he uttered an exclamation, and demanded: "Where did you get this ring?" his voice was agitated, and on my replying: "It belonged to a boy in New Venango," he started to his feet, crying: "In New Venango! Were you at Foster's? Did you see Harry? You spoke of a horrible hour; was there some misfortune?"

"It was an accident in which my brave Swallow and I were nearly burned alive," I said, extending my hand for the ring.

"Wait; I want to know how you came by this," he said. "I have a sacred right to it; greater than any one's else."

So he knew Harry and Foster, and must stand in some peculiar relation to them. I had a hundred questions on my tongue, but silenced them, and told him from the beginning the story of the night in which New Venango was destroyed. As it proceeded Old Firehand's excitement grew past control. He came closer and closer to me; his mouth hanging open as though he would drink in my words; his eyes fastened on mine, and his body bent as though he were on a horse's back, urging him forward. He struggled with me in the water, and as I described leaping the cliffs, seized my arm in such a vise-like grip I could hardly restrain an expression of pain, while the breath came loud and panting from his heaving breast.

"Heavens!" he gasped, falling back white and trembling as he heard how I had cleared the precipice, and brought the boy through in safety. "That was horrible, frightful! I have suffered as though my own body was scorching. Yet I knew you had saved him, or he could not have given you his ring."

"He did not give it to me; it fell from his finger without his knowledge."

"And you didn't give it back?"

"I couldn't; he ran away from me. I followed him the next morning, but he was with some people who had escaped, and who would not let me come near them; they accused me of causing the whole tragedy, and shot at me, so naturally I left them to themselves."

"I see. What became of Foster?"

"I heard that none but those people with whom I saw Harry had escaped."

"That was a horrible punishment for keeping back the oil to force the price up."

"Then you knew Foster?" I said.

"I have been in New Venango sometimes. And you are sure Harry was not hurt at all?"

"Quite sure. He is an unusual youngster."

"Yes. His father is an old trapper whose bullets know the way between the ribs of a foe."

"Where is his father?"

"Sometimes here; sometimes there. I dare say you'll meet him."

"I should be glad to."

"You will, I'm sure. You've earned his thanks."

"Oh, I didn't mean that."

"I know, I know. I understand you pretty well. Here's your ring. I'll send Winnetou in; his watch is up. Lie down and rest; we've a long ride before us. Good night."

"Good night. Don't fail to wake me if you need me."

"Sleep, young man; I can at least keep my eyes open for you. You've done enough for me."

He left me to speculate on the meaning of these last words. Long after Winnetou had come in, and wrapped himself in his blanket to sleep. I lay wakeful; it had driven all sleep from my eyes to re-live that awful evening, and it seemed to me that I still felt the hot breath of the flames around my head. Toward morning I slept, and when I awoke I was alone, though the others could not be far away, for the little kettle of boiling water hung over the fire, and the preparations for breakfast were making. I looked out, and saw my comrades standing talking earnestly together, and their glances toward our camp showed me that I was the subject of their conversation.

We resumed our journey that morning, and it seemed to me as we rode that there was something like tenderness in Old Firehand's eyes as he looked at me. During our noon halt, while Old Firehand had gone ahead to reconnoiter the surroundings, Winnetou laid his hand on my shoulder, and said: "My brother is as bold as the great cat of the forest, and as silent as the mouth of the rocks. He has ridden through the flaming oil, and has not spoken of it to Winnetou, his friend."

"The tongue of man," I answered, "is like the knife in the shield; it is sharp and keen, and not fit for playing."

"My brother is wise and right, but why has he not spoken of the boy that Swallow bore through the flames?"

"It would have sounded like self-praise. Do you know this boy?"

"I have borne him in my arms; I have shown him the flowers of the field, the trees of the forest, and the stars of heaven. I have taught him to shoot the arrow from the bow, and mount the wild steed. I have taught him the speech of the red men, and at last gave him the pistol whose bullet pierced Ribanna, the daughter of the Mascaleros."

I looked at him in wonder, and a suspicion dawned upon me which I could not verify, for Old Firehand returned at that moment. But I pondered on Winnetou's words, and putting them together with what Harry had said, and Old Firehand's manner and words, I thought I had the clue to the mystery.

After an hour's rest we again set forth, and our horses trotted on as though they knew that rest and oats awaited them, and as twilight began to fall the height behind which lay the valley wherein was Old Firehand's stronghold was already rising beneath our feet. We entered a ravine that apparently would land us in a river flowing by, for it seemed to have no other outlet.

"Halt!" cried a voice in the darkness. "Give the word."

"Brave and silent," said Old Firehand, responding with the countersign. On receiving it the sentinel came forth, and the sight of him filled me with amazement. Under the melancholy droop of a felt hat whose color, age, or shape no mortal man could determine, rose a nose of truly gigantic proportions, from a forest of beard. On each side of this great organ twinkled two little eyes of unusual brightness and restlessness. The head rested on a body invisible to us below the knees, the upper part of which was clad in an old leather hunting-jacket, apparently made for a much larger person, and which gave the little man the appearance of a child who had dressed up in his grandfather's dressing-gown. He carried an old gun which I would have handled only with the greatest caution, and as he stood before us in conscious dignity one could not imagine a droller caricature of a trapper than he. Funny though he might be I was delighted to see him, for he was Sam Hawkins.

"Sam, what's the matter with your eyes that you challenge me for the countersign?" asked Old Firehand.

"Well, a body's got to challenge somebody if he's a sentinel. Welcome home. I'm out of my wits with delight at seeing my tenderfoot again, and Winnetou, the great Apache chief."

He seized both my hands, and pressed me against his hunting jacket, quite trembling with joy.

"It does my heart good to see you again, dear Sam," I said. "Didn't you tell Old Firehand that you knew me, and had been my teacher in the chase?"

"Of course I did."

"And yet he never told me that I'd meet my old friend here."

Old Firehand laughed. "I wanted to surprise you," he said. "You see I have known you for a long time. You will find two other friends with me."

"Dick Stone and Will Parker then, for they and Sam are inseparable."

"The very ones, and they'll be glad enough to see you," said my host. "What's the news, Sam? How are the traps?"

"All right; come, see for yourself."

We turned to the left, where there was a narrow cleft, its opening overgrown with ivy and wild blackberry vines. Old Firehand bent low in his saddle, and we followed, riding slowly through the bed of a brook which flowed through this second, smaller ravine. For a long time, and with many turns, we followed our guide in the darkness, till at last we came to a similar cleft to that through which we had entered, and at its opening I paused in surprise. We found ourselves at the beginning of a valley surrounded by hills, whose sides were impassable cliffs. The valley was verdant, and many horses and mules grazed there, guarded by numerous dogs of that wolf-like variety which is used by the Indians as watch-dogs and beasts of burden.

"This is my 'village,'" said Old Firehand turning to us. "Here I dwell as in a castle. Not many of the redskins who crawl over those rocky hills suspect that these sharp rocks are not a solid mass, but enclose such a lovely valley."

"How did you discover such a valuable place?"

"I followed a raccoon to the cleft which was not then covered with ivy, and of course I immediately took possession of the place."

We pushed on further, and were immediately surrounded by Old Firehand's people, who gave full expression to their pleasure at his return. Among them I found Dick Stone and Will Parker, who were nearly beside themselves with delight at seeing me again, and whom Winnetou greeted cordially. Winnetou took off his horse's saddle and bridle, and gave him a light stroke as a suggestion to him to get his own supper. I followed his example, gave my fine Swallow full liberty, and then went off to see the place.

I had made the tour of the valley, and came back to the camping place, eaten my supper, and listened to self-laudatory stories of adventure till I tired, and rose up to make a little visit to Swallow.

I walked through the tender grass over which the clear and brilliant heavens spread so kindly, while its million lights looked down sadly on a world whose sons stood armed against one another. A soft, joyous whinny came from a bush which grew beside the brook, calling me to Swallow, who had recognized me, and rubbed his head lovingly on my shoulder. He grew dearer to me every day, and I laid my head lovingly on his soft, glossy neck. A quick sniffing of his nostrils, which I had learned was a warning, made me look around. Was I dreaming or awake? There stood Harry.

"Harry, is it possible?" I cried joyfully.

The boy acted embarrassed, remembering how we had parted. "I wanted to see your Swallow, who saved my life," he said.

"Here he is. Then you would rather not see Swallow's master?" I turned as if to go, but he laid his hand on my sleeve.

"Forgive me," he said. "I did not understand. And now you have twice put your life in the greatest danger to save my father. I must thank you, and beg your pardon."

"It's all right, Harry; you did not see straight, that's all. And as to the other cause for gratitude, any frontiersman would have done what I did; it's not worth talking about. Have you been doing any more wonderful shooting with your old pistol?"

He drew the weapon, and held it up. "You're a famous shot," he said; "but you couldn't do much with this old fellow. Queer you spoke of it, because my father and Winnetou said I should tell you its story."

"Wait a minute," I interrupted. "Then Old Firehand is your father?"

"Didn't you know that? Of course he is. But about this pistol. It was given me by Winnetou, and one of its shots entered my mother's heart."

I uttered an exclamation of horror.

"Yes," Harry said, "and it shall avenge her in my hands. Come over here and sit down. You must know about it, but it's a story to make short."

He sat down by me, and looking over the peaceful valley before us, began: "My father was born in Pennsylvania. He came West when he was quite young, and hardships and adventures of all sorts made him into a man respected by all the white settlers, and feared by the Indians. His wanderings brought him to Rio Pecos when Winnetou was a child, and he was the guest of Tah-tsche-tunge, the brother of the chief Intschu-Tschuna, and he learned to know Ribanna, his daughter. She was as beautiful as the dawn, and lovable as the mountain rose. None of the other daughters of the tribe knew so well how to tan the skins, and make the hunting clothes, and when she went to bring wood for the fire of her kettle, she stepped across the plain like a queen, and her hair fell to her feet in long strands. She was beloved by Manitou, the Great Spirit, and was the pride of the tribe, and all the braves longed to take her in their wigwam as their wife. But none found grace in her eyes, for she loved the white hunter, who was her father's guest, and he loved her, and spoke to her as to the daughters of the pale-faces. So they were married, and I was born in a happy home. As I grew older Winnetou, the son of my mother's uncle, and then about as old as I am now, taught me all that I longed to know of hunting, and games of courage and daring. I grew to be a boy of seven, and there came a day when my father went away, taking me with him, and when he came back his home was burned, his wife and little baby gone. Tim Finnerty, a white man, who had often been in the Apache pueblo, had wanted the rose of Rio Pecos for his wife, but the Indians were not friendly to him, for he was a thief, and so he vowed vengeance. He learned from my father, whom he had met in the Black Hills, that Ribanna was his wife, and he stirred up the Black Feet to go on the war-path against my father's camp. They did as he wished. While he was away they plundered and burned the camp, and carried off his wife and child. When he returned Winnetou was with him. They looked on the ruin before them, and followed up the trail of the robbers, and as the crime had been committed only the day before their return, they knew they would overtake them. Winnetou kept at my father's right hand, and I shall never forget the look on their faces, as they hastened on their way with agony in their hearts. We overtook them at Bee Fork, and waited until night to fall upon them. I was to stay behind with an Apache left to watch the horses, but he paid no attention to me, and when the moment of attack came I crept forward between the trees, and reached the edge of the wood as the first shot was fired. It was a horrible sight, the savages rushing at their enemies, while the groans of the wounded and dying filled the air. I laid in the wet grass praying, and after a while I crept back in terror to the watch. He had disappeared, and as I heard the triumphant howls of our foes I knew we were conquered. I hid until the following evening, and then ventured out. It was profoundly still, and the moon shone down on the lifeless forms lying there. I wandered between them, fascinated by my fright, and came upon my mother, shot in the breast, her arms clasping my baby sister, whose little head was cleft by a knife. The sight robbed me of my senses; I fell fainting upon them. How long I had lain there I do not know when I heard stealthy steps near me, and rose up to see my father and Winnetou, their clothing torn, and their bodies bleeding from their wounds. They had been taken prisoners, but had escaped."

Harry drew a long breath at the end of this tragic story, which explained to me all that I had been wondering over. He was Old Firehand's son, Winnetou's cousin, and the reason for their hatred for Paranoh, or Tim Finnerty, was only too plain. Harry had spoken like a man, and it was hard to realize he had been a little child when this tragedy was enacted. He turned to me and said: "Is your mother still living?"

"Yes."

"What would you do if she were murdered?"

"I would let the arm of the law seize the murderer."

"Good! But when it is too weak, or too short, as it is in the West, we have to make our own arm the law."

"Never forget the difference between punishment and revenge, Harry. The former is the consequence of sin, and is included in the idea of divine and human justice, but the latter is hideous, and lowers the human being to the level of the brute."

"You speak thus because you have no Indian blood flowing in your cold veins. The only feeling in the heart of my father and Winnetou as they laid the two innocent dead in their grave, was fierce hatred for Tim Finnerty, and that feeling I shared. You have slain the murderer of Ribanna, and you have saved her husband and son; forgive my being so unjust to you."

"There is nothing to forgive, my dear Harry. But you have not yet told me how you came by this pistol."

"When Finnerty shot my mother with it Winnetou threw himself upon him, and wrenched it away. He concealed it in the grass, and when I was old enough he gave it to me, to avenge her death with it. You have done it for me." he put his long brown fingers in my hand as I held it out to him, and we rose, and went back to the camp.

CHAPTER IX

PARANOH COMES TO LIFE AGAIN

I OPENED my eyes in the morning to see Harry standing in my doorway." Sam Hawkins and I are going to look after the traps; will you come with us, Mr. Hildreth?" he said.

"With pleasure, only call me Jack, for I'm not so very venerable, and life's too rapid out here for ceremony," I said, jumping up.

We went out through the cleft in the rocks, turning toward the direction in which we had come yesterday. We waded the little stream downward in its course to the point where it flowed into the river. Thick briars that were really impenetrable grew on the banks of the stream, and the tendrils of the wild grape twined themselves together, reaching over to the trees, and forming a net-work through which we had to cut our way with a knife. Although no danger was to be anticipated, yet Sam, going on ahead, scanned every spot where a footprint might be discovered, and his little eyes ceaselessly turned from side to side, peering through the rich young vegetation. At last he lifted a branch, stooped down, and crawled under. Harry did the same, saying to me: "Come this way; this is our beaver path."

A small but perfectly distinct line ran through the thicket, and we crept for some distance parallel with the stream till Sam paused, and turning to us, laid his fingers on his lips.

"We are there," whispered Harry, "and the sentinel is suspicious."

After a time, during which it was profoundly still, we crept forward and reached a bend of the stream, which enabled us to watch the beaver colony. A dam about the width of a man's foot had been thrown out in the stream, and its four-footed owners were busy strengthening and increasing it. On the opposite bank I saw a crowd of industrious furry folk, gnawing the branches with their sharp teeth where they must fall in the water. Others were occupied transporting these branches, shoving them ahead of them as they swam, while others plastered their structure with rich loam which they brought from the shore, using their feet and thick tails as trowels. I watched the labor of these active little people with interest, especially one unusually big specimen sitting on the dam with the air of a sentinel. Suddenly the thick fellow pricked up his ears, half-turned, uttered a cry of warning, and the next moment disappeared under water. Instantly the others followed him, splashing the water in their sudden plunge with their flat tails. There was not time to be amused by their movements, for this unexpected disappearance meant the approach of an enemy, and the greatest enemy of these peaceable little animals is man.

As the last beaver plunged into the water we had our weapons in our hands, waiting the appearance of the intruder. We had not waited long before we saw two Indians creeping along the stream a little above us. One had several traps hung over his shoulder, the other carried a bundle of skins; both were fully armed, and looked around with an air that showed us they knew they were near an enemy.

"Confound them!" hissed Sam through his teeth. "They've found our traps. Wait, you curs, and my old gun Liddy shall tell you whose those traps and pelts are."

He raised his gun, but it was important that we should punish these fellows without noise, and I caught the trapper by the arm. I saw that they were Poncas, and the war-paint on their faces showed they were not out hunting, but were on the war-path. There were others then in the vicinity, and a shot would summon their avengers.

"Don't shoot, Sam," I whispered. "Don't you see they're on the war-path, and there are more near here? Take your knife. I'll attend to one, and you to the other."

The two Indians stood facing us, looking for footprints. Softly, very softly I crept forward, my knife between my teeth. When I reached the edge of the bush I sprang out, and used my knife so effectually on the Indian nearest me that he fell without a sound. It was necessary to do this, for they were Poncas, and if they discovered our stronghold it would cost us our lives. I drew out my knife, and turned, ready to attack the other if needed, but he lay on the ground with Sam standing astride of him, saying: "Now, young man, you may take as many skins in the Happy Hunting Grounds as you please, but you can't have ours!"

"We must hide these Indians' bodies, Sam," I said.

"You're right. I'll bet my moccasins to dancing pumps there'll be red men here in a little while."

Accordingly we concealed the bodies of the Indians, and while Sam returned to the valley to warn our people, Harry and I crept forward in the thicket to discover how the land lay. We made our way onward for an hour without interruption, and came to a second beaver colony, but its inhabitants were not visible outside their dwellings.

"Here was where we put those traps that the Indians stole. You see the trail leads into the woods from here; we must follow it," whispered Harry.

"I wish you would go back, and let me do this alone, Harry," I said.

"How can you think of such a thing?" asked the boy.

"Do you realize how dangerous it may be?"

"Why shouldn't I? It can't be more so than the things I have done already. I'm going anyhow, so don't bother."

We went on then, leaving the stream, and stepping softly between the slender trunks of the tall forest which formed a thick green roof over the moss-grown earth, in which we could see the trail only by the closest scrutiny. Harry, who had gone ahead, stopped. The trail was no longer that of two, but of four men, who had come to this point together, and had separated here. The two whom we had disposed of had been so fully armed that I concluded a large number of their tribe was near, such as could only be called out by an important enterprise, and it occurred to me that this undertaking might be revenge for our rescue of the train.

"What shall we do?" asked Harry. "This new trail leads to our camp, which we mustn't expose to discovery. Shall we follow that one going there, or keep on with the big trail?"

"This fourfold trail leads to the redskins' camp, who have hidden, of course, to wait the return of their spies. Before all things we must seek that out to find out their number, and intentions. The entrance to our little stronghold is guarded by a sentinel, who will do his utmost to keep our secret, and we must leave it to him."

"You are right; let us go on."

The woods extended from the height in which the valley began, considerable distance in the plain, and was cut through with deep, rocky furrows in which grew ferns and wild berry vines. As we approached one of these depressions I noticed a smell of something burning, and looking sharply for its cause, discovered a thin cloud of smoke rising from the crown of trees on the edge and which was often interrupted or entirely disappeared in fluttering pennons. This smoke could only come from an Indian fire, for while the whites throw their wood on the flames in its full length, thus getting a broad, high flame which makes a smoke that often betrays them, the savage uses only the ends of chopped wood, and gets a little flame, with scarcely perceptible smoke. Winnetou used to say that "the white man made his fire so hot that he could not sit by it to get warm."

I held Harry back, and bade him hide behind a bush while I took a peep at these people.

"Why shouldn't I go too?" he demanded.

"One is enough, and two doubles the risk of discovery."

He nodded assent, and slipped cautiously into his hiding-place, while I, keeping concealed from tree to tree, crawled up to the furrow whence the smoke had come. Sitting, or rather lying on the ground, closely huddled together, was such a crowd of Indians that the eye could scarcely penetrate its masses. At the exit of the camp were sentinels, perfectly unconscious of my proximity. I tried to count them, and had run my eye over half of them, when I stopped in utter amazement. Nearest to the fire sat -- could it be possible? -- the white chief Paranoh, Tim Finnerty. I had seen his face so plainly by the light of the moon on the night when I thought I killed him, that I could not be mistaken, and yet I could not trust my eyes, for the scalp lock which I knew was hanging on Winnetou's belt apparently was back again on his head.

The sentinel who stood nearest me turned toward the place where I lay concealed, so I slipped back, signaled Harry to follow me, and returned to the place where the trail divided. From here we followed the new tracks which led through the thickest growth of foliage straight to the valley. It was clear to me now that the Poncas had been reinforced and were following us step by step for revenge. Our delay during Old Firehand's illness had given them time to call together all their available force. But why they had gathered such a force against three, why they had not fallen upon us long ago, instead of letting us withdraw peacefully I could not understand, unless Paranoh knew of the trapper colony, and meant to destroy it. There was no trouble in keeping this trail, and we made good time into the valley. We met Sam Hawkins near its entrance, and when I told him what I had seen, he shook his head dubiously. "It will cost powder, my boy; much powder. I came along with my pelts to the brook, and I plainly saw two redskins spying around the edge of the bushes, scarcely eight feet away. I got under cover, and let them go ahead, one up and one down the valley. I bet they got a warm reception. I've been waiting here ever since to ask them, politely, what they had seen."

"Do you think they will come back this way?"

"Sure. If you want to be sly you'll go over to the other side, so we can catch them between us."

I followed this suggestion, and Harry and I took up our position directly opposite to Sam, and waited the return of the Indian spies. Our patience was well tested. Fully an hour passed before we heard the soft fall of a gliding step. It was a weather-beaten fellow, who could scarcely find room at his belt for the scalps he carried. As soon as he was within reach I sprang out, and settled him, as we did his companion who appeared shortly, and then we returned to the village.

Old Firehand heard my story to the end in silence, but when I told him of Paranoh an exclamation of surprise, and of joy too, escaped him. "Is it possible you weren't mistaken?" he asked.

"Only his hair makes me doubtful."

"Oh, that proves nothing. Sam Hawkins is an example of a man's living through scalping, and it's quite possible your aim was not quite true that night. His people found him, and took him away. While I was recovering, he was getting well too, and he has watched us, and followed us. Are you tired, Jack?"

"No."

"I must see the man myself; will you go with me?"

"Of course I will, only I must remind you of the danger in going. The Indians after waiting in vain for their spies to return, will come out to look for them. We may be cut off from our own people."

"It's possible, but I can't wait here quietly till they find us. Dick Stone, get your gun; we're going to look for redskins. Harry, stay with Will Parker, and look after the guns while we're gone."

Harry begged to be allowed to go with us, but his father would not hear of it, and we set out through the bed of the brook. Winnetou had left the camp shortly after our early start for the traps, and had not returned. He would have been the most welcome addition to our party of three, and I could not help feeling a little anxious about him, for he too might have encountered the Indians, and alone. Even as I was thus meditating a bush in front of us parted, and the Apache stood before us. Our hands, which at the first rustle of the branches had sought our weapons, relaxed as we heard him say: "Winnetou will go with his brothers to look for Paranoh and the Poncas." We looked at him in surprise.

"Has my brother seen the warriors in their camp?" I asked.

"Winnetou must watch over his brother, Old Shatterhand, and over the son of Ribanna," he replied. "He went behind them, and saw their knives pierce the hearts of the red warriors. Paranoh has taken for his own the hair of a son of the Osages. His hair is a lie, and his thoughts are full of falsehood."

I scarcely heard his last words, for at that very moment I saw two eyes gleaming behind the bushes, and with a quick spring had seized the man to whom they belonged. It was he whom we sought Paranoh! As I tightened my fingers around his throat there was a rustle on both sides, and a band of Indians sprang out to help their chief. My friends had seen my movement, and were ready for my assailants. I had the white chief down with my knee on his breast, the fingers of my left hand around his neck, and the right holding his hand which had seized his knife. He squirmed under me like a worm, trying to throw me off. Bracing his feet, he tried to raise himself; his long false scalp lock lay beneath him, and his bloodshot eyes rolled in their sockets; he foamed at the mouth with rage, and the head stripped by Winnetou's knife swelled and pulsated with his struggles. I felt as though I had a raging beast under me, and choked him till he drew himself together convulsively, his head dropped, his eyes closed, with one last shudder his limbs stretched out -- he was conquered.

Rising, I looked around upon a scene that no pen could ever describe. None of the combatants had any other weapon than a knife or tomahawk, except Dick Stone. Not a man stood upright, but all were struggling and twisting on the ground in his own blood, or his opponent's. Winnetou was about to plunge his knife into a foe whom he had overcome, and did not need me. Old Firehand lay on one of his assailants, trying to keep off a second who had wounded him in the arm. I hastened to his assistance, and knocked the Indian down with his own tomahawk, which he had dropped. Then I went to Dick Stone, who lay between two dead Indians under a gigantic man who was striving with all his might to deal him a fatal blow. He did not succeed; his comrade's tomahawk, which I had just used, put an end to his attempt. Stone arose, and straightened himself. "By George, that was help at the right time; three against one is tough. Much obliged."

Old Firehand too stretched out his hand to me, and was about to speak when he discovered Paranoh. "Tim Finnerty? Is it possible? Who did him up?" he exclaimed.

Winnetou answered for me: "Old Shatterhand overcame him. The Great Spirit has given him the strength of the buffalo that ploughs the earth with his horns. But Paranoh's people will come after him, and my brothers must quickly follow Winnetou to the valley."

"He's right," said Old Firehand, from whose arm the blood was streaming. "But we must first remove the traces of this fight. Go ahead, Dick, and see we're not surprised."

"I will, only take this knife out of my flesh first, will you? I can't do much with this thing in me." One of his foes had stabbed him, and during the struggle the blade had been driven farther in. Fortunately it was not in a dangerous spot, and when it was withdrawn left a wound that to Dick's cast-iron constitution was a mere trifle.

"How shall we take our prisoner away?" asked Old Firehand after we had done what was necessary, and recalled Dick.

"That's simple enough," said Stone. He cut off a quantity of withes from the roots near us, took off Paranoh's coat, cut it into strips, and nodding to us with satisfaction, said: "Make a drag, and bind the darling on it fast, and haul him along."

We followed his suggestion, and soon were under way, Winnetou coming behind to remove the broad track this invention left. Yet though we reached the valley safely, and with Old Firehand's mortal foe a prisoner in our hands, we felt, Winnetou and I at least, that we had not seen the last of our enemies the Poncas.

CHAPTER X

A DOUBLE CAPTURE AND A DOUBLE RESCUE

EARLY the following morning, when I went out to give Swallow my usual greeting, I found all my friends discussing the place and manner of Paranoh's execution. With a sense of dramatic fitness, Old Firehand wanted to take him to Bee Fork, where his wife and baby had been murdered, and put him to death there. It seemed to me the risk of being overtaken by the Poncas which they would incur in going so far, and delaying so long, was not worth running. I saw that Winnetou agreed with me, but Harry fiercely opposed my counsel, and prevailed with his father, whose wishes coincided with the boy's. The result was that the little band set forth, and I, who refused to have anything to do with this expedition, because they meant to torture the criminal, remained behind in charge of the valley. Winnetou went with the others, chiefly to protect Harry.

Only a few of the trappers stayed at home, among them Dick Stone. The sentinel assured me he had seen no sign of danger, but I had learned to trust only my own eyes, and I searched the place thoroughly for a trace of an Indian. Just at the entrance to our valley I noticed some broken twigs, and on close examination saw that a man had lain here. Some one had spied upon us then, and any moment might bring an attack. And there was another danger. He might have seen Paranoh and his escort go away, and it was important above all things to warn Old Firehand. Consequently, when I had told our sentinel of my discovery, I set out upon the trail of my friends. I had not gone far before I came on a second trail, coming sidewise from the bushes, and leading in the direction of Bee Fork. I followed it as cautiously as possible, yet so rapidly that I was not long reaching the spot where the waters of the Bee Fork flow into the river. As I did not know the place where the execution was to be I had to redouble my caution. The trail led me around a bend of the river, and I saw a clearing, in the middle of which was a group of fir balsams under whose branches sat the trappers in lively discussion, while the prisoner was bound to the trunk of one of the trees. Directly before me, at the most eighteen feet distant, lay a small band of Indians, and I saw in a moment that the rest had gone around to the right and left to attack my friends from three sides, and drive them into the river. There was not a moment to lose. I pressed the trigger of my rifle. For the first few seconds my shots were the only sound, for friends and foes were equally surprised by the unexpected thwarting of their plans. But immediately the war-cry of the Indians arose behind each bush, and the clearing was full of howling, shrieking, panting men, struggling in a mad hand-to-hand conflict.

I had sprung out at the same time the Indians had, and was just in time to save Harry from an Indian who had attacked him as he was about to shoot Paranoh. The trappers stood with their backs against the trees and were defending themselves desperately. They were seasoned men, who had fought many a hard fight, and did not know fear, but it was plain that the superior force must prevail. One of the Indians had at once freed Paranoh. He swung his arms around his head to set the blood in motion, snatched a tomahawk from one of his followers, and growled as he rushed at Winnetou: "Come, you dog of a Pima. You shall now pay for my scalp." the Apache, hearing himself saluted by the nickname of his tribe, hopped, but he was already wounded, and was threatened at the same time from the other side. Old Firehand was surrounded by enemies, and we others were so hard pressed that we could not help. Longer resistance in this case were the greatest folly. Therefore I cried, as I seized Harry in my arms: "Into the water, men, into the water," and set the example myself.

My voice was heard above the din of combat, and those who could obeyed it. Though the Fork was deep, it was so small that only a few strokes were necessary to reach the other shore, but of course we were not safe there long, and my object was to cross the point, and swim over the big river.

I signaled to Harry to do this just as Sam Hawkins' little figure appeared, and started for the willows with the same end in view. But Harry held back, crying in anguish: "Father, father! I must go to him. I can't leave him."

"Come," I said forcing him onward. "We can't save him if he has not already saved himself."

We rushed on through thick and thin to reach the camp as soon as possible. Only a part of the Indian force had been at Bee Fork, and since we had been discovered, and spied upon in our stronghold, it was likely that those we had left behind had also been attacked.

We had made considerable of the distance when we heard a shot in the direction of the valley. In a moment it was repeated, then several shots rang out; there was no doubt that the trappers left behind were fighting the Indians. We pressed forward eagerly to help them, and in spite of the obstacles in our path, reached the valley in a short time. We stopped at the point overlooking the entrance, where I had discovered the Indians' trail. They lay hidden in the edge of the woods, besieging the water gate from there, and to get any result we must go around behind them. Just then we heard a rustling as though some one were rushing through the bushes. At a sign from me we all hid behind the thick foliage of a shrub, and waited the appearance of the new-comers. How great was our delight as Old Firehand, followed by Winnetou and two trappers, came in sight! They also had escaped, and Harry showed his joy in this meeting in a way to prove to me that he had more heart than I had credited him with.

"Did you hear the shots?" demanded Old Firehand hastily.

"Yes."

"Come then. We must help our folks, for though the entrance is so small that one man can guard it, we don't know what may have happened."

"My white brothers may stay here. Winnetou will go to see on which tree the scalps of the Poncas hang." without waiting for an answer to this proposition the Apache went away, and there was nothing for us to do but await his return, during which time two more of our people joined us, drawn hither by the shots, as we had been.

A long time passed before Winnetou returned, but when he came we saw that he had a fresh scalp at his belt; he had surprised an Indian, and we could no longer stay where we were, for when the Poncas discovered the death of their comrade they would know that we were behind them. We followed Old Firehand's suggestion, and formed in a line parallel to the edge of the bushes, to attack our foes from the rear. We made our guns, which were wet from their bath, ready for use, and having come into position, at a signal, one after another, the nine guns rattled. Each shot found its man, and a howl of surprise and terror filled the air. Our line was so stretched out, and our shots followed one another so fast that the savages thought our number greater than it was, and took to flight.

Victorious we returned home, and made ready for further developments. One of the trappers was stationed as sentinel, the others attended to their wounds, and settled down to supper and rest. Gathered around the fire each one had to recount his experience during the trying day, and all rejoiced that the Indians had been driven off, and had abandoned the assault. Even Old Firehand shared this opinion; only Winnetou differed from it. He lay by his horse, a little at one side, and seemed sunken in profound thought.

"The eyes of my red friend are gloomy, and his brow bears the mark of care. What are the thoughts of his heart?" I asked, going over to him.

"The Apache chief sees death coming through the gate, and ruin descending from the hills. The valley is red with the flames of fire, and the water is crimson with the blood of the slain. Winnetou speaks with the Great Spirit. The eyes of the pale-faces are blinded by hate, and their wisdom has disappeared in their desire for revenge. Paranoh will come, and take the scalps of the hunters, but Winnetou is girded for combat, and will raise the death song over the bodies of his foes."

No one seemed impressed by this prophecy, though I had long since learned to trust Winnetou's foresight. As evening came on, however, our precautions were doubled, and at my request I was put on guard just before dawn, the time when the attack was most likely to be made. Night rested calm and still over the valley, and the fire threw its quivering light around us. Swallow, who was allowed to roam at will in the hill locked pasture, was out of sight; I went to look him up, and found him quiet at the foot of the hills. After we had greeted each other as affectionately as usual, I went on still further, for a faint, falling sound made me listen. The horse too raised his head, and as the least breath might betray us, I laid my hand over his spreading nostrils. I listened, but beyond that fall of a stone there was nothing stirring. Perhaps some one besides myself had noticed that, and waited to be sure it had not been heard. This theory was the right one, for after a long time I saw several figures rise from the dark rocks, and descend beneath them, and soon I saw a number of Indians coming over the brow of the hill, one behind another, following their leader with cautious steps. In a few moments they would be in the valley. If I had had my Henry rifle I could have given the alarm, and made an end of Paranoh, who was the leader, but unfortunately I had only my revolver in my belt, and it was no good for long range. Just then I heard a shot at the entrance of the valley, quickly followed by more, and I saw at once that the Indians were feigning an attack at that point to call our attention from the real source of danger. I sprang up the hill to get at Paranoh, and was so near that I could almost touch him, when the mass of stone beneath me gave way, and I fell from rock to rock, from ridge to ridge, all the way down, and for a moment lost consciousness. When I could collect myself, and open my eyes I saw three Indians only a few feet away from me, and jumping up, though I was fearfully bruised and shaken, I fired my revolver at them, sprang on Swallow, and tore back to the fire.

The Poncas, who now saw that their plan was discovered, raised the war-cry, and pursued me.

I found our camping place deserted; the men had gathered at the entrance, but had turned back at the sound of my shots.

"To the heights," I shouted. "The Indians are inside."

It was the only hope of deliverance, but it was too late. Hardly had I spoken when we were surrounded. It was a wild, a horrible struggle, such as no imagination can paint. The half extinguished fire threw its flickering light over the foreground of the valley, in which groups of men were fighting like demons. Through the howls of the Indians rose the trappers' cries of encouragement, and the short, sharp crack of revolver shots, while the earth seemed to tremble under the feet of the combatants.

There was no doubt that we were lost. There was no possibility of anything favorable happening to us and we felt our moments were numbered. But we would not die like sheep; we would defend ourselves to the last, and with that coolness which gives the civilized man such an advantage over the savage.

I thought of the dear ones at home, to whom I should never return, but I put the thought away, for it would not do to think of anything that would make me falter. I tried to ask God to have mercy on my soul, and looked anxiously to see how many of my friends were still on their feet. Scarcely two paces from me on my right was Old Firehand. The way he fought for his life with his foes pressing on him filled me even then with wonder. His long gray hair hung in matted locks over his shoulders, his extended legs seemed rooted in the ground, and with a heavy tomahawk in one hand, and a sharp knife in the other, he held at bay the force pressing on him. He had more wounds than I, but none had brought him down, and once more I admired his tall, erect figure.

Just then Paranoh appeared, forcing his way to us. As soon as he saw Old Firehand, he cried: "At last I've got you! Think of Ribanna, and die."

He pushed by me, but I seized him by the shoulder, and prevented the deadly blow he was about to inflict.

"You too?" he cried." I'll have you alive. Give him a lariat."

Springing past me before I could again raise my tomahawk, he drew his pistol; the shot whizzed by me.

Old Firehand threw up his arms, sprang forward convulsively, and fell without a sound. I felt as though the bullet had entered my own breast as I saw the hero fall. I knocked down the Indian who was attacking me, and was about to fall on Paranoh, when I saw a dark form forcing its way through the enemy, and raise its supple arms in front of the murderer. "Where is the crow of Atabaskah? Here stands Winnetou, the chief of the Apaches, to avenge his white brother."

"Ah, you Pima! I'll settle you!" Paranoh cried, but I heard no more. I had been too interested in the scene to remember myself. A lasso fell over my neck, and at the same time I felt a tremendous blow on my head, and lost consciousness. When I came to myself it was perfectly dark and still around me. A burning pain in my head at last recalled to me the blow I had received, and all that had preceded it. I thought I heard some one breathing beside me.

"Is any one here?" I asked.

"Well, yes; the man asks as if Sam Hawkins was nobody."

"Is it you, Sam? Where in the world are we?"

"Under shelter, boy. They have stuck us in this hole where we buried the skins. Lucky thing we removed them! At least they haven't found those."

"And how about the others?"

"Old Firehand is dead, Dick Stone is dead, Will Parker is dead. All are gone, but you and Winnetou, and the little fellow is half alive, and Sam Hawkins is not quite done for."

"Are you certain that Harry is alive, Sam?"

"Do you suppose an old scalper doesn't know what he sees, man? They have stuck him in another hole beside us with your red friend. They are lovely people these Poncas, sweet things! They have taken everything away from this old 'coon, everything; pistol, pipe, and Liddy's gone up the spout -- poor Liddy -- but I kept my knife; stuck it up my sleeve."

"You have your knife still?" I cried. "Yet what good can it do?"

"We'll see. We might wriggle along by rocking ourselves till we got together."

We tried this experiment, and it was successful. Although my hands were bound, I managed to pull the knife down from Sam's sleeve, and cut the ropes on his arms with it. Sam's hands being free the rest was simple, and in a few moments we stood erect, free in every limb.

"That's a brilliant stroke, Sam Hawkins. You seem to me not such a bad fellow," said the little man, figuratively patting himself on the back.

"Now the first thing is to see our surroundings, Sam, and get weapons," I said. We went to the door, and drew aside the skins which curtained it.

"Do you see something, Master Jack?" whispered Sam. "As sure as I'm alive that thing leaning against the stone there is my Liddy!"

I was so glad to see Swallow standing near, safe and sound with Winnetou's horse, and Paranoh's chestnut, that at first I could hardly enter into the little man's joy.

"Sam, can you be depended upon?" I whispered.

"I don't know who knows that if you don't."

"You go to the right, and I will go to the left. Then cut Winnetou's and Harry's bonds quick. Are you ready?"

He nodded, with an expression on his face that promised success. "Now then."

We glided behind the two Indians guarding the prisoners, and came up to them unobserved. Sam stabbed one with such sure aim that he sank without a sound.

I, being unarmed, had to first snatch the other one's knife, but seized his throat as I did it, and the cry he would have uttered died out in a faint gurgle. A few rapid cuts freed the prisoners.

"Here, take weapons," I cried, seeing escape was impossible without them, and forcing the gun of the Indian I had killed into Winnetou's hands.

"Swallow, Swallow," I called, and the horse obeyed my voice. In an instant I was on his back, saw Winnetou mount his own, and Sam take Paranoh's.

"Come here quick in heaven's name," I cried to Harry, who had started after a horse. I seized his arm, swung him over my saddle, and turned toward the gate of the valley through which Sam had already disappeared.

It was a moment of the wildest excitement. Howls of rage filled the air, shots rattled, arrows whizzed around us, and through it all echoed the neighing of the horses on which the savages threw themselves. I was the last of the three, and could never say how I came through the narrow, winding pass without being overtaken by the enemy. Just as we were about to go around the bend a shot rattled behind us, and I felt Harry droop. He was wounded. "Swallow, my Swallow, go on," I urged the beast in anguish, and just as he had borne me away from New Venango, he now rushed onward.

The warm blood ran from Harry's wound over the hand with which I held him. "Can you hold out the rest of the way?" I asked.

"I hope so."

Again I urged the horse onward. He proved worthy of his name, for he skimmed on like a swallow, his feet scarcely seeming to touch the ground. As I looked around I saw Paranoh close behind me, and even in that brief glance could distinguish the mad fury with which he pursued us, and redoubled my calls to the brave horse, on whose speed and endurance everything hung. Suddenly I saw Winnetou dismount, and take his stand behind his horse, as he loaded his captured gun. I followed his example, and laid Harry in the grass. There was no time for me to load, for Paranoh was too near, so I seized my tomahawk. Our pursuer marked our motions, but carried away with rage rushed on me, swinging his tomahawk. Then Winnetou's shot rang out. Our foe drew himself together convulsively, and fell from his horse. Winnetou turned over the lifeless body with his foot, saying: "The snake of Atabaskah will sting no more, nor call the Apache chief a Pima My brother may take back his weapons."

True enough; "the snake" carried my knife, tomahawk, revolver, and Henry rifle, and Winnetou's silver studded rifle hung at his saddle.

We rescued our property, and with Harry in my arms I once more remounted Swallow, while Winnetou sprang upon his chestnut. We did not relax our speed, and after a time all our pursuers were left behind us. The day was won.

As soon as possible we returned to the valley. We found Sam Hawkins there before us, and the anxiety I had felt for him was set at rest. One more joy awaited us as the crown of that crowded day. Winnetou went over to where Harry knelt by his father's body. The weeping boy held his father's head on his breast while the Apache examined the wound. Just as I came over to them I heard Winnetou exclaim: "Ugh, ugh, ugh! He is not dead; he lives!"

CHAPTER XI

A TRADER IN COUNTERFITS

THREE months passed in quiet and the effort to recover lost ground after the events set down in the last chapter.

The hope of saving Old Firehand which Winnetou's words had awakened, was fulfilled, but his convalescence was very slow; even at the end of this long time he was not able to stand. Harry's injury proved trifling; Winnetou was wounded in many places, though not dangerously, while my wounds did not bother me much, for I was getting as hardened to pain as an Indian. Sam had come out best of all, but the grief of the faithful little man over the loss of his comrades Dick and Will counted for more than mere physical pain.

It had been decided that as soon as Old Firehand was well enough for the journey he should settle down in the East with Harry, for he was too old a man ever to recover sufficient strength to resume his life of a trapper. Harry too would be better off where he could be properly trained and educated. But in order to do this he must first dispose of a quantity of skins which he had accumulated, and we were at a loss how to bring it about, when we opportunely heard of a trader beyond the hills who would probably buy them.

The next difficulty was how to get at this man, which I solved by offering to go for him, and Winnetou insisted on accompanying me, for the region through which I must pass was infested with hostile Indians. It was the third day after our departure when we reached that part of the country where he would be likely to be met with. Should we find him? If he were among the Indians we must be extremely cautious, but there were also white settlers' houses scattered along at intervals through this region, and we determined to try to discover one of these, and there ask for information of our trader.

Just as it was getting toward night, and we were beginning to give up hope of a house that day, we saw a field of rye, surrounded by other fields of grain. Beside a brook whose waters flowed into a river, rose a strong, rough block house, with a garden enclosed by a stout fence, and an enclosed clearing where horses and cows were grazing.

We turned in here, dismounted, tied our horses, and went toward the house, which had little gun hole windows. From two of these we saw double-barreled guns pointed at us, and a harsh voice called out: "Stop! Stay where you are. This is no inn; what do you want?"

"We come from Old Firehand, and we want to know where we can find a certain trader."

"Go look for him. You've got an Indian with you, and in these times no one lets in people of that color."

"You'd be honored by a visit from this Indian; he is Winnetou, the Apache chief."

"You don't say so! I wonder if that's so! In that case you must be Old Shatterhand."

"That's precisely who I am."

"Then come in, quick. Such people as you are most welcome. You shall have everything you want I can give it to you."

The guns were withdrawn, and the settler appeared in a moment at the door. He was a big-boned, strong old man, who, one could easily see, had found life a struggle. He shook hands heartily, and led us into the house where his wife and two sons were sitting. "You mustn't take it ill that I spoke somewhat roughly at first. We have to be on the lookout for Indians, and few white men come here who haven't been driven out of the East. But this makes us all the more glad to see the other sort. So you're after a trader?"

"Yes."

"Do you want to do business with him?"

"Yes; I want to sell a lot of skins to him for cash."

"Well, I know the man, and the only one hereabouts."

"Is he honest?"

"Oh, honest! What do you call honest? He's in business for what he can make; if you let him get the best of you it's your own fault. He's called Burton, and has four or five agents. One of 'em's staying here tonight; he'll be here soon. His name's Davis. Hark! I hear some one now."

A horse's hoofs sounded outside, and our host went out to meet the newcomer, with whom he presently returned. "This is Mr. Davis, who, as I told you, is Burton's agent," he said.

The trader was a middle-aged man of ordinary appearance with nothing striking about him either in a good or a bad sense, yet I did not quite like the expression with which he looked at us. He did not seem as glad to see us as he should be, considering the profit likely to be derived through meeting us. He had as good a supper set before him as we had already done justice to, but he did not seem very hungry, and soon rose from the table, and went out to look after his horse. I cannot call it exactly mistrust, but it was something very like it that made me follow him. His horse was tied in front of the house, but he was nowhere to be seen. After a long time I saw him coming around the corner of the fence, and when he saw me he stood still for a moment, and then came toward me quickly.

"You like moonlight walks, Mr. Davis?" I asked.

"No; I'm not so romantic," he replied.

"Yet you go rambling off alone."

"But not for love of the moon. I don't feel just right; I've had indigestion all day, and long sitting in the saddle has made it worse. I had to move around a little."

He untied his horse, and led him into the enclosure with ours, and then joined us in the house. He was his own master, and why should I bother about what he did? Still, the reason he had given me for his moonlight promenade was rather flimsy.

We discussed business until we went to bed, and he showed such knowledge of skins, and seemed so square that even Winnetou approved him, and talked to him more than was his wont with strangers. It was arranged that he was to go with us in the morning to look at the skins, and estimate their value.

We set out in the early dawn, and Davis fell behind us like a footman, which we thought rather queer, but we were glad to have him do so, as it left us free to talk without restraint. We went back the way we came, but although we knew the region perfectly, we had to keep a sharp lookout for the trails of men and beasts, either of which might prove dangerous. It was owing to this that we fell on a trail that otherwise might have escaped us, for great pains had apparently been taken to conceal it. While we were examining it Davis came up, and also sprang from his saddle.

"Is this an animal, or a man's trail?" he asked.

Winnetou did not answer, so I said: "You can't have had much experience in reading such records, or one glance would have answered your question. It is the trail of men."

"I should think it would be plainer if there were horses."

"Yes, but there were no horses."

"No horses! I don't see how a man who wasn't mounted could exist in this region."

"Did you ever hear of a man losing his horse?"

Winnetou cut this conversation short by asking: "Does my brother Old Shatterhand understand what this means? They are three pale-faces without horses; they have no guns, but carry sticks. They have gone on from here stepping in each other's footprints, and the last one has tried to wipe out the tracks; they seem to have feared being followed."

"But isn't it curious to find unarmed white men here in this dangerous section, unless they have been robbed?

"My white brother has reached my own conclusion. These men lean heavily on their sticks; they need help."

"Does Winnetou wish to find them?"

"The chief of the Apaches is glad to help any one who needs him, and never asks whether he is white or red. We will go after them."

We remounted, but Davis grumbled, saying complainingly: "Why shouldn't we leave these people to themselves? It can't do any good to go after them."

"Not to us, certainly, but it may to them," I said.

"But we waste so much time."

"We're not so pressed for time that we must refuse help when it is required," I answered sharply.

Davis muttered something in his beard, and threw himself on his horse. I had very little confidence in him, but it never occurred to me that he could be the wretch he was.

The trail led us into the open Savannah, and soon we saw those whom we sought. They stood still when they first caught a glimpse of us, as if they were afraid, and then ran for their lives. We easily overtook them, being mounted, and called out to them reassuringly. They were entirely unarmed, and one had his head tied up, another carried his arm in a sling; the third was uninjured.

They told us that they had been attacked by Indians early in the previous day, had lost their horses, and were in constant dread of another meeting with the savages. As their way lay with ours we proposed that they should travel with us, and gave them food, and sat down with them while they ate, and rested.

As they had no horses they would necessarily retard our progress, and Davis seemed highly displeased with our arrangement, but we did not stop to ask his opinion, though his unsympathetic behavior made me dislike him more than ever, and watch him more closely. The result of this observation was most unexpected.

I noticed that when he thought no one saw him a scornful smile passed over his face, and he would hastily glance at Winnetou and me. I saw too that when he caught the eye of one of our new companions a quick glance passed between them, and it seemed to me they had a secret understanding. Did they know one another? Was the trader's sullen manner merely a mask? What reason could they have for deceiving us? The men we had rescued were certainly under obligations to us. Could I be mistaken?

The wonderful sympathy, the interchange of thought and feeling between me and my Apache brother showed itself anew. Even as I was puzzling over this problem, Winnetou dismounted, and said to the oldest man, who called himself Wharton: "My brother has walked long enough; he must take my horse. Old Shatterhand will gladly lend his also. We are well, and strong, and can easily keep up with the horses." Wharton protested against this kindness, but was none the less glad to accept it, and his son took Swallow. Winnetou and I fell behind too far to be overheard, and were careful besides to use the Apache tongue. "My brother has given up his horse less from compassion than for some other reason," I began.

"Old Shatterhand has guessed it."

"Have you too been watching these four men?"

"I saw that Old Shatterhand was suspicious, and kept my eyes open. I have seen that the strangers are not wounded, and as their bandage and sling is a lie, so is it a lie that they were attacked by Indians. Does my brother Old Shatterhand think that this trader is their enemy?"

"No, he is feigning."

"Yes; I too saw that. He knows them, and perhaps belongs with them."

"Shall we tell them to their faces what we think of them?"

"No, for their secret may have some reason that does not concern us. In spite of our mistrust of them these four men may be honorable ones. We could not tell them that we thought they were bad."

"Sometimes my brother Winnetou shames me. He is often more kind and tender-hearted than I am."

"No one should give a man pain unless he deserves it. It is better to suffer an injustice than inflict one. There can be no motive for Davis to treat us badly, for his employer will make a good trade with Old Firehand. It may be that they are all traders, and mean to rob us after they are in the valley."

"Winnetou has had the same thought I have; I believe that is their scheme. We must watch them day and night."

"Yes, for it is certain their horses are near here. Only one of us may sleep; the other must watch, and yet not let these people see it."

Winnetou's keenness had discovered the truth, but not all of it. Had we guessed it we should hardly have remained so cool, and continued to tolerate our companions.

We should have preferred camping that night on the open prairie, where we could see on all sides, but a strong wind arose, bringing rain with it, and we were obliged to seek shelter in the woods.

After we had eaten our supper our companions showed no inclination to sleep, but entertained one another with stories, even Davis becoming talkative, and relating adventures he had met with in his wanderings. It struck me there was some object in this sociability; was it to distract our attention? I looked at Winnetou, and saw that he had the same thought, for he had laid all his weapons ready to hand, and kept a sharp lookout on all sides, though only I, who knew him so well, could see it. His lids drooped as though he slept, but I saw that he watched everything from under his lashes, and I did the same.

The rain ceased, and the wind died down. We lighted no fire, and sat with our faces turned toward the woods, whence, if there were an enemy, he would come. The slender sickle of the young moon arose, and shed its soft light over us through the tree tops. Winnetou lay stretched out in the grass, resting on his left elbow, his face pillowed in the hollow of his hand. I noticed that he slowly drew his right leg nearer his body, so that the inside of his knee made an angle. Could he be intending a knee shot, the most difficult of all shots? Yes, actually! He reached for the handle of his silver studded rifle, and laid it, as if with no special intention, in the angle formed by his knee. I followed with

Karl May

my eyes the direction in which it pointed, and saw under a bush in front of the fourth tree from us a soft phosphorescent light which would not have been noticed by a less experienced eye than the Apache's. It was a pair of human eyes watching us from the bush. Winnetou meant to shoot between them the only sure place and with the difficult knee shot. A little, little higher and the eyes were within range. I waited with strained expectation the next moment; Winnetou did not miss his aim, even at night, and in this way of shooting. I saw him lay his finger on the trigger, but he did not pull it. He lifted his finger, dropped his gun, and stretched his leg out again; the eyes had disappeared.

"A wise fellow," he said to me in Apache.

"At least one who knows the knee shot," I replied.

"He knows also that we saw him."

"Yes; more's the pity."

"I'll crawl after him."

"It's dangerous; let me do it, Winnetou."

"Shall I send you into danger I would avoid myself? My brother may help me get off so the spy will not suspect I am after him."

We waited a while, then I said: "Would you fellows mind keeping quiet? We start early, and need sleep. Did you tie your horse well, Mr. Davis?"

"Yes," he replied with a snarl.

"Mine is still free," said Winnetou aloud. "I will tie him now. Shall I tie my brother's with him?""

Yes, if you will," I answered, as if that were the real object of his going. He rose slowly, threw his blanket over his shoulder, and went out to where our horses were grazing. The interrupted conversation was resumed, at once to my annoyance and satisfaction. I could not hear what happened to Winnetou, but on the other hand it kept the man he was after from hearing him. I dropped my lids, and waited. Five minutes passed, ten, a quarter, yes, half an hour. I should have been worried about Winnetou, only I knew how long such a task as his required. At last I heard a step behind me in the direction in which he had gone. Turning my head a little I saw him coming; the blanket still hung over his shoulder, and I hoped he had dealt with our hidden foe. I turned my head back, and waited for him to take his place again beside me. The steps came nearer, paused behind me, and a voice that was not Winnetou's said: "Now this one."

Looking up I saw the blanket indeed, but he who wore it was not Winnetou, but a bearded fellow. As he spoke he raised the handle of his gun to strike me. Quick as a flash I turned aside, but too late; the blow fell, not on my head, but on my neck; a second stroke followed on my skull, and I lost consciousness.

When I came to myself, and with a great effort raised my heavy lids, I saw that it was dawn. It seemed to me I was dead, and my ghost listened from eternity to the speech around my body. I could not understand a word until I heard a voice whose tones would have waked me if I had really been dead, saying: "This dog of an Apache will say nothing, and I've killed the other one. What a nuisance! I meant to have had some fun out of him, and teach him what it means to fall into my hands."

That voice restored me completely. I stared at the man, whom I had not recognized in the first glance because of the beard he now wore. It was Santer!

72

CHAPTER XII

SANTER AGAIN

WHEN I grasped the fact that Santer actually stood before me I wanted to close my eyes, and let him think I was still unconscious, but my lids would not fall. I stared at him, unable to take my eyes away, till he saw it, and sprang up, crying joyfully: "He's alive; he's alive!"

He asked me a question, and as I did not answer it, he knelt down, seized me by the nape of the neck, and shook me, striking my head hard on the stones. I could not defend myself, for I was fastened so that I could not move a finger. Then he growled: "Will you answer now, you dog? I see that you can, and if you don't, I'll make you." as he shook me I had seen Winnetou lying at one side, fastened together in the form of a ring. Such a position would torture an India-rubber man; what must he be enduring?

I saw besides Santer, only Wharton, his son and nephew; Davis had disappeared. "Now will you speak?" demanded Santer threateningly, "or shall I loose your tongue with my knife? I will know whether you know me, and hear what I say?"

What use was silence? It could only make matters worse. I really did not know whether I could speak or not, but I tried, and in a weak voice said: "I know you; you are Santer."

"So you do know me," he stammered, mocking me.

"Are you very glad to see me? Are you perfectly enchanted to find me here? It's a glorious, delicious surprise for you, now isn't it?"

I did not answer this malicious question, and he drew his knife, set its point at my heart, and threatened: "Will you say yes, a loud yes, this moment, or shall I stab you?"

Then Winnetou spoke in spite of his pain: "My brother Shatterhand will not say yes; he will rather let himself be stabbed."

"Silence, dog," growled Santer. "If you say another word I will draw you up till your bones break. Now, Old Shatterhand, you friend whom I love with all my heart and soul, aren't you really overjoyed to see me?"

"Yes," I answered loudly, in spite of Winnetou's warning.

"You hear that?" asked Santer triumphantly of the other three. "Old Shatterhand, the famous, invincible Old Shatterhand, is so afraid of my knife that he says with his feeble tongue he is glad to see me."

Whether my previous condition had been less serious than it seemed, or whether this man's jeers effected a change in me, I do not know, but my head all at once felt as sound as ever, and I said, laughing in his face in my turn: "You are mistaken; I did not say that from fear, but because it is the truth. I really am glad that at last I see you again."

Though I laughed, I spoke so earnestly that he stepped back, elevated his brows, looked at me a moment searchingly, and then said: "That blow has shaken up your brains so that you are delirious. I might almost think the fellow meant that!"

"And so I do, entirely."

"Then you certainly are crazy."

"Not a bit of it; my head was never clearer."

"Then it's sheer, cursed impudence, and I'll draw you up like your friend, and hang you upside down till your veins burst."

"Nonsense! That's likely! In ten minutes I'd be dead, and you couldn't find out what you want to know."

I saw I had hit the mark. He glanced at the others, and said: "We thought this scoundrel was dead, when he was not even unconscious. He has heard all the questions I asked this cursed redskin, who won't speak."

"You're mistaken," I said. "I was unconscious, but Old Shatterhand has brains enough to see through you."

"Is that so? Then tell me what it is I want of you."

"Bosh; drop that child's play. You won't find out anything. I tell you I am really glad of this meeting. We have looked for you long; we can't help being glad. We have you at last, at last, at last."

"Don't be a fool; you are completely in our power; nothing can save you, unless I choose to spare you. It may be that I shall, but only in case you give me full information. Look at these three men; they belong to me. I sent them on to draw you into my trap. What do you think I am now?"

What he was I had long known very distinctly, but prudence forbade my answering categorically, so I contented myself with telling him that he was a scoundrel, and always had been.

"Good!" he remarked. "I'll let that insult pass now because my day of reckoning is coming. Now I know that you, or rather Old Firehand, have a lot of skins for sale. I have seen the settler with whom you stayed, and I know all about it. You did not find the trader you came to meet, but one of his agents. I came after you, and caught you. The trader, who I believe calls himself Davis, I'm sorry to say got away."

It seemed to me as he said this he glanced at the bush where he himself had hidden the night before. It was an involuntary glance, and struck me at once. Was there any connection between Davis and that bush? I must find out, though I could not look that way. He continued: "You know me; I know you, and we both understand that whoever falls into the other's hands is lost. I have you now, so your life is ended. The only question is how it shall end. I had determined to torture you as man was never tortured before, but now that I intend to discover Old Firehand's hiding-place, I'm not so sure. Tell me where this place is, and describe it to me exactly, and you shall have a painless death -- a bullet in the head."

"Very lovely! It's truly sweet and tender of you, but not very wise."

"Why?"

"We might describe the wrong place, to earn this quick death."

"I'm not so short-sighted as you think. I know how to test your information. But first I must know whether you will betray the place?"

"Betray is the right word, but you ought to know that Old Shatterhand is no traitor. I see that Winnetou has failed you; probably he has not answered you at all, for he is far too proud to talk to such a cur as you. I have spoken to you, however, for my own reasons."

"And you will tell me nothing?"

"Not a word."

"Then we'll fasten you in a ring, like Winnetou."

"Do it."

"And torture you to death."

"Which will do you no good."

"You think so? I tell you I will find that place in any case."

"Possibly, by some blind chance, but too late even if you do, for if we are not back at a certain time Old Firehand will remove the skins to a place of safety; we arranged that before we started."

He looked down darkly and reflectively, playing with his knife. I saw through his double plan. The first half had miscarried; he must now fall back on the second part of the program. At last he raised his head and said: "So, if you'll not do what I wish I will force you to it. We'll see if your limbs are as insensible as the Apache's." he signaled to the other three, who seized me, and carried me over by Winnetou. This gave me a chance to see the bush at which Santer had glanced. My suspicion was right; a man was hidden there. He raised his head to see what was to be done with me, and I thought I recognized Davis.

It is useless to dwell on the next three hours, during which I was bound into a ring, and Winnetou and I suffered side by side without speaking, or allowing our tormentors to hear a sigh. Every fifteen minutes Santer came, and asked if we would do what he wished, but he received no answer. It was a question of which would hold out longer, he or we. It was a little after midday that having again questioned us, Santer sat down with his comrades, and discussed something in a low tone. In a few minutes he said quite loudly: "I too believe that he is hidden somewhere about here, because he didn't get his horse when he escaped. Look all around carefully; I'll stay here with the prisoners."

Even if I had not known this was a farce, the loud tone in which he spoke would have shown it. As a rule one does not announce to a man that he is to be captured.

The three took their weapons, and withdrew. Winnetou whispered to me softly: "Does my brother know what is to happen?"

"Yes; they're going to capture Davis, and bring him here. Then they'll be very much surprised to find he is a friend of Santer's."

"Yes, and Davis will plead for us, and get our freedom. It will all be done as in those beautiful big houses of the pale-faces where men act plays."

"Exactly. Of course Santer is Burton, the trader, and Davis has led us into his hands." during this brief conversation we had not moved our lips, and Santer could not hear our soft whisper. He sat half turned from us, and listened. After some time a loud call resounded, two or three voices answered, then there followed a loud scream, and we saw the three Whartons come out of the bush, bringing Davis between them, apparently struggling to get away.

"Have you got him?" cried Santer, jumping up. "I knew he must be near; fasten him in a ring like --" he stopped short, started as though surprised, and then cried: "What! Who have you got there?"

Davis seemed equally delighted and astonished; he broke away from the three, crying: "Mr. Santer! Is it possible? Oh, it's all right then, and nothing will happen to me."

"Happen to you! No, I guess not. Who could have thought that you and the Davis I wanted to catch were identical? Are you too with Burton, the trader?"

"Yes, Mr. Santer, and I was going to do a good piece of business on this very ride, only last night we were attacked by --" he too stopped short. They had been shaking hands heartily, but now Davis drew back a little, and said: "It can't be you who attacked us, Mr. Santer?"

"It was."

75

"Good heavens! Attacked by a friend; a man whose life I have often saved! What made you do it?"

"How should I have known you were here?"

"You couldn't. But look at these men there, fastened, and in such a way! That mustn't be; I can't stand it. I will free them."

He turned toward us, but Santer seized his arm. "Stop! What are you doing?" he cried. "These two are my deadly enemies."

"Your enemies! That's bad, still I must help them. And think who they are: Winnetou and Old Shatterhand!"

"It's precisely because they are those two that they shall have no mercy from me."

"Even if I ask you it?"

"Even then."

"But think what you owe me; I have saved your life more than once."

"I know, and I won't forget it, Davis."

"Do you remember that the last time you swore to do anything I should ask of you?"

"I believe I did say so."

"And now I claim that promise."

"Don't do it, for I can't keep it. I am not willing to break my word."

"Come with me, Mr. Santer; I must talk to you." he took him by the arm and drew him aside, where they stood talking and gesticulating. They acted their farce so well that it would have deceived any one who was not thoroughly prepared.

At last Davis alone came to us, and said: "I have succeeded so far as to lighten your burden a little. You heard and saw what an effort this required; still I hope to free you altogether."

He unfastened us from our agonizing position, and returned to Santer to carry on his work of mercy. After a longer time they both came to us, and Santer said: "It seems as though the devil must protect you. I once made this gentleman a promise which I must keep. So I will do the most foolish act of my life, and free you, but everything you had with you, even your weapons, are mine."

Neither Winnetou nor I spoke.

"Well, are you too amazed at my generosity to speak?"

As no answer came to this either, Davis said: "Naturally this unexpected rescue has struck them dumb. I'll untie them."

He laid his hands on the ropes that held me. "Stop!" I said. "Either everything, or nothing, Mr. Davis."

"What do you mean?"

"We won't have freedom without our weapons, and all our property."

"Well, you're an ungrateful pair! I try to save you, and this is your return!" he drew Santer away again, and Winnetou whispered: "That was well done. It is certain they will do as we require, for they expect to get everything back later."

This was what I thought, and it proved true, for at last they all came over to us, and Santer said: "You have simply superhuman luck. My promise forces me to do what I know is idiotic. You'll laugh at me, but I'm the last man to laugh at, as you'll find out later. I'll set you free this time, and you shall have all that belongs to you. Till evening, however, you are to be tied to this tree, so that you can't follow us till early dawn. We'll ride back, and take Mr. Davis with us, so he can't free you before the appointed time. When it is dark he shall come back to you. You owe him your lives; see that you repay him."

No one spoke again. We were fastened side by side to two trees, our horses tied near us, and our weapons laid beside us. When this was done the five men rode away.

After a long silence Winnetou said: "We must catch Santer. Which does my brother think the surest way to do it?"

"Not by entrapping him in Old Firehand's valley."

"No; he must not learn the hiding-place. Davis will ride behind us to give him secret signs how to follow. When the right time comes we will disable him, and ride back on our track to wait for Santer. Does my brother agree to this plan?"

"Yes; that's the best I know of. Santer expects to get us, but we will get him."

"How!" Winnetou made no other reply, but the tone in which he spoke this one word expressed his satisfaction that after such a long vain search, at last; at last, his foe would fall into his hands.

The day crept like a snail, but evening finally came, and as soon as it was dark we heard a horse's hoofs, and Davis came to untie us. Of course he did not fail to lay full weight on the fact that he was our deliverer, and we tried to act as though we believed him, and expressed our profound gratitude. Then we mounted, and rode away.

Davis kept behind us, and occasionally we heard his horse prancing, which left a deep trail, and as the young moon arose we could see that from time to time he broke off a branch and dropped it to mark the way unmistakably. At noon of the next day we made a long halt of three hours, and rode two hours more, when we decided the time had come to deal with Davis. We reined up, and dismounted. He too sprang from his horse, and asked: "Why do you stop? This is the third time today. It can't be far now to Old Firehand's. Won't you go on, instead of camping for the night?"

Winnetou said: "No rascal can go to Old Firehand's."

"Rascal! What does the chief mean?"

"I mean that you are one."

"I? Since when has Winnetou been so unjust to a man who has saved his life?"

"Saved it! Do you really think you could deceive Old Shatterhand and me? We know everything. Santer is Burton, the trader, and you are his spy. You have left signs for him to follow all the way. You are to deliver us over to Santer, yet you pretend you saved our lives. We watched, and now our time has come."

He stretched out his hand toward Davis, who took in the situation, turned, and swung himself into the saddle like a flash. But I had the horse by the bridle as quickly, and Winnetou had sprung up behind him, and seized him by the neck. Davis, who saw in me his most dangerous assailant, as I held his horse, drew his pistol, and aimed at me. I bent down as Winnetou seized the weapon. Both shots went wild, and a moment later Winnetou had Davis off his horse; another half moment and he was bound and gagged. We bound him with the thongs which had fastened us, disarmed him, and tied his horse near by, intending to come back after we had captured Santer. Then we rode back on our own trail, and hid behind the trees to wait for Santer. A quarter, a half, another quarter of an hour passed, and he did not come. After an hour I saw something moving across the horizon, and in a moment Winnetou pointed to it, and said: "Ugh! A rider."

"Surely a rider. That's strange."

"Ugh, Ugh! He rides at a gallop in the direction in which Santer must come. Can my brother see the color of his horse?"

"It seems to be a brown."

"It is brown, and Davis' horse was brown."

"Davis! Impossible! How could he get away?" Winnetou's eyes flashed; his breath came quicker; the light bronze of his face grew darker, but he controlled himself, and said calmly: "Wait one more quarter of an hour."

The time passed, but did not bring Santer. Then Winnetou asked me to ride to Davis, and see if he were still there. I did as he asked. The man was gone, and his horse also. Winnetou sprang to his feet as if shot from a cannon when I returned and reported this misfortune. "He has gone to warn Santer," he cried. "Who set him free? Did you see any trail?"

"Yes; a rider had come from the east; it was he freed him."

"Who could it be? A soldier from the fort?"

"No; the footprints were so large I am sure they were Sam Hawkins'. And I thought I recognized the hoofs of his mule Nancy."

"Ugh! There may be time to catch Santer, though he is warned. Let my brother come."

We threw ourselves on our horses, and rode westward like the wind. Winnetou did not speak, but a storm raged within him. Woe to Santer if he caught him! We came on Davis' trail, and in three minutes reached the spot where he had met Santer. They had turned back in the direction in which Santer had come. Had they kept on in the old way we could have followed them in spite of darkness, but they were too wise for that, and had branched off in another direction. It was too dark to see. Winnetou turned his horse, and we galloped back without a word. Once more Santer had escaped us; was it for today, or forever?

The moon was high as we reached the river, and entered the ravine. We met Sam Hawkins just at the mouth. "Were you riding today, Sam?" I asked.

"Yes; I went out a piece to look for you; we were getting anxious."

I was right; Sam, usually so wise, had been stupid enough to set Davis free.

"Does my white brother know what he is?" asked Winnetou, generally so considerate, and gentle towards the feelings of others.

"A frontiersman, and a trapper?" answered Sam innocently.

"No; no frontiersman, nor trapper, but such a thickhead as Winnetou has never seen before, and will never see again. How!"

CHAPTER XIII

HELLDORF SETTLEMENT

WE set out the following morning, Winnetou and I, in pursuit of Santer. We hoped to overtake him shortly; we certainly did not dream that we should spend nearly a year in this pursuit, nor that the parting from Old Firehand was forever. We left Sam Hawkins there with the understanding that if we were not back before Old Firehand was ready to go East, he should make his way to Rio Pecos, where he could get tidings of us. For ten whole months Santer eluded us. Our wanderings took us from Mexico to the North West, and the adventures we met with in their course would fill more than one book, but this is the story of Nugget Mountain, and they cannot be told here. At last we had a clue to the murderer's whereabouts that led us back to the Sioux country, and we were following it with no less earnestness of purpose than when we had set out a year and a half before with the sorrow of the death of Intschu-Tschuna and Nscho-Tschi fresh in our hearts.

At that time the West was infested with lawless men, the refuse and scum of the East, who were a perpetual menace to the young settlers, and to the camps of workmen engaged on the railroads. We had with us now a young settler named Fred Walker, who had suffered from these men, and who had joined us because there was so much likelihood of travelers meeting these outlaws, as well as hostile Indians in that section.

As evening closed in around us we reached the brow of a hill, and were about to descend on the other side, when Winnetou, who rode ahead, reined up and pointed onward. We looked in that direction, and saw a grassy plain on which was encamped a large band of Indians. They had been preparing meat, for the skeleton of a buffalo lay on one side, and ropes on which hung thick pieces of buffalo steak drying had been drawn between poles. Winnetou scanned the camp sharply." thirty two tents; two hundred warriors," he said.

"And there are white men with them," I added.

The Apache pulled out the field glass which I had given him, to look more closely. "Ko-itse, the liar and traitor," he muttered. "Winnetou will plant his tomahawk in his skull."

I looked through the glass with much interest. "Ko-itse" means Firemouth, and the bearer of this name was known throughout that section as a good orator, a daring warrior, and an implacable foe of the whites.

"My brothers may wait; Winnetou will find a place for them and him to hide." he disappeared underneath the trees, and soon returned to lead us along the top of the hill to a place where the trees were so thick one could hardly penetrate them. Inside the grove there was room for our horses to move about, and we lay till dark, ready to spring out at the slightest sound.

When night had really closed in we left Fred with the horses, and went out, Winnetou to the right, I to the left, to spy on the Indian camp, and try to learn something of their intention. The wind was against me, which gave me an advantage over Winnetou, as there was no fear of my being discovered and betrayed by the horses. Half an hour passed, and at last I lay behind the buffalo skin tent of the chief. There were five white men and three Indians around the fire. The former talked loudly together, while the more cautious Indians communicated rather by signs than words. One of the whites was a big, bearded man, with a scar on his forehead as if from a knife wound.

"And how far is it from here to Echo Canyon?" one of the men asked him.

"It is easily reached in three days' march."

"And how many people are employed there, Dawson?"

"About a hundred and fifty, all well armed. Besides there are valuable stores, and plenty of drinking saloons. It's worth going for. We'll start early in the morning, go a piece northward, and then divide into bands going in different directions, and unite at Green Fork; we'll be at Echo Canyon in four days. Even if all the workmen are in, we needn't worry; we outnumber them, and before they can grab their weapons the greater part will be done for."

I could not positively have had a better moment for spying than this. I had learned far more than I expected to, and there was nothing to keep me there longer, for I knew all there was to know, and any moment might betray me. Very slowly and carefully I crawled back, and when I reached the edge of the woods I put my hands to my mouth, and imitated the croak of the bull-frog, which was the signal between Winnetou and me. I wanted to recall him, for the work was done.

I was glad enough to get back to our thicket, and to Fred, who was as glad to see me. "Tell me what you discovered," he said. "I am burning with curiosity."

"Well, burn a little while longer till Winnetou comes; I can't tell my story twice."

At last we heard the bushes rustle, and Winnetou laid down beside me. "My brother Jack gave me the sign; was he successful?"

"I heard all we want to know."

"My brother is always fortunate in spying on our enemies. He may tell me about it."

I repeated what I had heard. "Now," I said, as I ended, "we can't let such a thing be done without an effort to stop it. We'd share their guilt if we let this rabble fall on those honest men who are building the railroad."

"That's so," assented Fred heartily. "But how shall we stop it?"

"There's no need of asking. We'll go ahead, and warn the people who are to be attacked."

"Ugh!" cried Winnetou, starting to his feet. "Let my brothers go now."

He untied his horse, and we did the same, led the beasts out of the thicket, and rode away. It was a dark, starless night, and only a Westerner would undertake to ride through such a difficult country. An Eastern man would have led his horse, but the denizen of the Wild West knows that the beast can see better than he. Here Winnetou showed his powers. He rode over brooks and crags, over stock and stone, and not for a moment was he doubtful of the direction to take. Swallow was his usual trusty self, and even Fred's old Victory, though she sometimes neighed her disapprove, kept step with us.

When dawn broke we found ourselves ten miles away from the camp of the Ogellallah Sioux, and by the next day had put forty miles behind us, and were delighted with old Victory's pluck. We rode just before sunset between two hills close together, looking for a suitable camping place. Suddenly the hills separated, and we found ourselves on the side of a rock-bound valley, in the midst of which was a little lake, fed by a stream flowing from the east, and leaving the lake again to flow out through the rocks on the west. As we saw this valley we paused in surprise, not because of the valley, but what it contained. Among its bright verdure wandered horses, sheep, goats, cows and children. Five big block houses, with out-houses stood at the foot of the hill, and just above on a cliff stood a little chapel, over which rose a carved wooden crucifix. Beside this chapel there were several people who did not seem to see us. They looked toward the west where the golden ball of the sun was every moment sinking lower, and just as it touched the river whose waters were tinted with its glorious color, there pealed from above the silver voice of a bell. Here in the Wild West, in the midst of the forest, a crucifix! Between the war-paths of the Indians a chapel! I took off my hat, folded my hands, and said the Angelus.

"Ti-ti -- What is that?" asked Winnetou.

"That is a settlement," answered Fred sagely.

"Ugh! Winnetou sees the settlement, but what is that sound?"

"That is the vesper bell; it rings the *Ave Maria.*"

"Ugh!" repeated the Apache. "What is vesper bell? What is the *Ave Maria?*"

As the last peal of the bell died away a hymn rose softly on the sunset air. I listened, amazed at the words. It was a little hymn I had written when in college, and sent to a Catholic magazine:

> "Now the light of day is fading,
> Night enfolds us, still and gray;
> Would that grief, our poor hearts lading,
> Might with daylight steal away.
> Mary, Mother, interceding,
> Lay our sighs before God's feet;
> While thy children humbly pleading,
> From their loving hearts repeat:
> *Ave Maria.*"

It was really my *Ave Maria*; how did it get here on the edge of the Rocky Mountains? The simple, touching melody flowed down over the valley like a dew from heaven; it overcame me completely. My heart seemed to expand to infinity, and the tears fell on my cheeks.

As the last note died away over the valley I snatched my gun from my shoulder, fired twice, and spurring Swallow, clattered down toward the settlement, and over the river without stopping to see whether my companions were following. The two shots had not only wakened the echoes of the valley, but recalled it to life. The doors of the houses opened, and everybody came out to see what it meant. When they saw a white man, they were reassured, and waited my coming quietly. Before the door of the nearest block house sat a little old woman. Her garments were simple and clean; everything about her spoke of hard work, but over her face framed by its white hair, played a sweet smile of that contentment which can only be possessed by a soul which lives in an unshaken trust in its God.

"Good evening, grandmother. Don't be afraid; we are honest men. May I dismount?" I said.

She nodded smilingly: "Welcome, sir, in God's name. An honest man is always welcome. There is my oldest son, and my Will; they will look after you."

The singers had come down from the chapel, attracted by my shots. They were a lusty graybeard; beside him a younger man; behind them six others of varying ages, and all had the strong, hardy bearing of backwoodsmen. The oldest extended his hand to me, and greeted me cordially. "Welcome to Helldorf Settlement, sir. It's a pleasure to see a stranger."

I sprang from my horse, and shook his hand. "Thank you; there's no pleasure in life like the sight of a kindly face. Have you a night's lodging for three tired riders?"

"Of course we have. My name's Hillman, and this is my son Will."

"And I'm Jack Hildreth at home, and out here I'm Old Shatterhand. The other two coming along now are Fred Walker, a frontiersman, and Winnetou, the Apache chief."

"Is it possible? I've heard of him a hundred times, and always the finest things," cried Hillman. "And are you Old Shatterhand? I won't tell you what I've heard of you."

"There's one thing you can't have heard, and that is that I wrote that *Ave Maria* you sing. I never was more surprised than in hearing it here."

When I said this the entire little community hardly knew how to show their pleasure, and give me welcome. To these simple people the author of a hymn must be a very great and learned man indeed, and I was relieved that Winnetou and Fred came up just then to rescue me from their embarrassing enthusiasm.

The elder Hillman greeted Winnetou as cordially as he had me, and the Apache responded with less reserve than he usually showed. A friendly contention arose as to who should entertain the guests, which Hillman settled by saying: "They dismounted before my house, and they all belong to me."

In the block house we were received by a pretty young woman, Will's wife. As we sat at supper the elder Hillman told us how they came there and bought this land, because they had heard that precious stones abounded in that region, and he was a stone cutter by trade. They had been disappointed, and though they lived peacefully, and contentedly, still the failure to find gems where they had sunk all their little capital had left them poor. Winnetou knew every angle in the mountains of the West, and though I knew that an Indian very rarely and unwillingly speaks of the treasures of the hills, I resolved to lay the case before him, and I did so, speaking in Apache.

He looked thoughtfully before him, then his dark eyes rested on our hosts, and at last he said: "Will these men fulfill a wish of Winnetou's?"

"What is it?"

"If they will sing again what Winnetou heard from the hill as we came, he will tell them where they can find stones."

I was astonished to the last degree. Had the Ave Maria made such an impression on him that to hear it again he was willing to betray the secret of the hills?

"They will sing it," I said, having appealed to them.

"Let them look in the Gros Ventre hills; there is much gold. And in the valley of the Beaver River, where its waters flow into the Yellowstone Lake, there are many such stones as they seek."

While I repeated this to the settlers, and explained the location of these two points, the neighbors came in, and interrupted us. By degrees the room filled up, and we spent such an evening as I had never had in the West. They sang all kinds of songs, for they were of German blood, and feasted in music.

Winnetou listened silently, and at last asked: "When will these men keep their promise?"

I reminded Hillman of it, and they began the *Ave Maria*. They scarcely had started to sing than Winnetou stretched out his hands, and cried: "It does not sound well in the house. Winnetou will hear it on the hill."

"He's right," said Will. "It should be sung in the open air. Come outside."

The singers went up the hill a little way, while we remained in the valley. Winnetou stood beside me, but soon disappeared. Then from the darkness floated down in sweet pure tones:

"Now the light of day is fading,
Night enfolds us, still and gray;
Would that grief, our poor hearts lading,
Might with daylight steal away."

We listened in silence. Darkness veiled the singers, and it was as if the hymn came from heaven. When it was over we all went back to the house, but Winnetou was missing. More than an hour passed, and he did not come, so I went to look for him, asking that no one follow me unless he heard a shot. I found him beside the little lake, sitting as still as a statue. Softly I came up to him, and sat down beside him without speaking. For a long time the silence was unbroken, then he raised his arm, and pointed to the water, saying: "This lake is like my heart."

I was afraid to speak, and he relapsed into silence, and when he spoke again it was to say: "The Great Spirit is good; I love Him."

Again I feared to disturb his thoughts by a word. In a little while he spoke again: "My brother Jack is a great warrior, and wise in council; my soul is like his own, but I shall not see him when I enter the Happy Hunting Grounds." this was said so sorrowfully that it was a new proof to me how dear I was to Winnetou.

"Where is my brother's heaven?" he asked.

"Where are the Happy Hunting Grounds of my friend?" I answered.

We had been comrades for nearly two years, and stood by one another through danger, joy and sorrow, yet never had the promise I had given him to be silent in regard to my faith been broken. I knew that he appreciated this, and that now when he himself had broken this silence, what I said would have double effect. "Manitou is the Lord of all things," I continued. "But let my brother consider which is the true God, the Manitou of the red man, or the white man's God. The white man says He is Father of all, red and white alike, and calls them at last into eternal blessedness and love. But the red man thinks Manitou commands him to kill all his foes, and after a life of fighting he goes into that gloomy Hunting Ground where murder begins anew. Which is true?"

Winnetou was silent. After a time he said: "Why are not all white men like my brother Jack? If they were Winnetou would believe their priests."

"Why are not all red men like my brother Winnetou?" I retorted. "There are good and bad men among all races. The earth is far more than a thousand days' ride long, and quite as wide. My friend knows only a little corner of it. The whites rule over it all, except a few small places, in one of which, where my brother lives, the wicked pale-faces, whom the good turn away, take refuge. This is why Winnetou thinks there are so many wicked pale-faces. My brother wanders through the hills; he hunts the buffalo, and kills his foes; is there happiness for him in this? Does not death lurk for him behind each tree and bush? Has he ever been able to give all his love and trust to an Indian? Is not his life all labor, care, vigilance and suspicion? Does he find rest, peace, confidence and refreshment for his weary soul under the ugly scalps, or the treacherous camps of the wilderness? But the Savior of the white men says: 'Come to Me, all ye who labor, and are heavy burdened, and I will refresh you.' Why will not my brother go to that Savior, as his brother does?"

"Winnetou does not know Him," he said simply.

"Shall I tell my dear Winnetou about Him?" I asked.

His head sank, and after a long pause he said: "My brother Jack has spoken truly. Winnetou has loved no man like him; Winnetou has trusted no man but his friend, who is a pale-face and a Christian. My brother knows all lands, and their dwellers; he knows all the books of the pale-faces; he is daring in combat, wise at the council fire, and gentle to his enemy. He loves the red man, and studies his good. He has never deceived his brother Winnetou, and today also will tell him the truth. The word of my brother is worth more than the word of all the medicine-men. The red men howl and shriek, but the white men have a music that comes from heaven, and echoes in the heart of the Apache. My brother may explain to me the words these men sang."

I began to explain the *Ave Maria*. Then in simple words, my voice full of my love for him, and longing to teach this noble soul as it should be taught, I told him the faith of the pale-face. Winnetou listened speechlessly.

When I ended he sat a long time in profound silence. At last he rose, stretched out his hand to me, and said with a long sigh: "My brother has spoken words which can never die. Winnetou will not forget the great, good Manitou of the pale-faces, the Son of the Creator, who died on the cross, nor the maiden who dwells in heaven, and hears the hymn of the settler. The faith of the red man teaches hatred and death; the faith of the white man teaches love and life. Winnetou will choose between life and death. I thank my brother Jack. How!"

We returned to the block house where they were becoming anxious about us. We slept in Hillman's soft bed, and in the morning parted from the worthy people with hearty gratitude, and with the promise to return if we could do so. They accompanied us a short distance, and before we said good-by the eight singers drew aside, and again sang the Ave Maria for the Apache.

When they had finished it, he gave his hand to each one, and said: "Winnetou will never forget the voices of his white friends. He has sworn never again to take the scalp of a pale-face, for they are the sons of the good Manitou, who loves the red men too."

And so we rode away to save the camp of the railroad builders at Echo Canyon. The last ride, but one, alas, that I should ever take beside my friend, my devoted Winnetou.

CHAPTER XIV

AT ECHO CANYON

WE rode through a small ravine between the great rocks that were the mouth of Echo Canyon. The first workmen we came to were busy blasting, and did not see us for a moment; when they did look up, and saw three strangers armed to the teeth, and one an Indian, they promptly dropped tools for weapons. I waved my hand to them, and galloped toward them.

"Good day," I cried. "Put down your guns; we are friends."

"Who are you?" asked one.

"We are hunters, and have important news for you. Who is in command here?"

"Engineer Colonel Rudge, but he's away. You must see Mr. Ohlers, the paymaster."

"Where is Colonel Rudge?"

"He has gone after a band of wreckers, who derailed a train. You'll find Mr. Ohlers beyond in the camp, in the largest house."

We rode in the direction indicated, and after five minutes came into the camp. It consisted of some block houses, and two rough stone ones. Around them was a wall of stones loosely piled together, but which seemed strong, and was about five feet high.

We dismounted, and entered the largest of the buildings. Its interior consisted of one room, in which were a number of chests and sacks, showing it to be the supply depot. There was only one man there, a little dried up creature, who rose from a chest as we came in. "What do you want?" he asked sharply as he saw me. Then he discovered Winnetou, and shrank back in horror. "Oh, Lord-a-mercy," he cried. "An Indian!"

"Don't be alarmed, sir," I said. "We're looking for Mr. Ohlers, the paymaster."

"I'm Mr. Ohlers," he said, with a frightened glance from behind his big steel spectacles.

"We wanted to find Colonel Rudge, but since he is away we must tell you our errand."

"Speak," he said, edging toward the door.

"When did Colonel Rudge go away?"

"What do you want to know for?" he asked, and suddenly slid out the door. The big iron hinges rattled, it slammed again, the bolt groaned. We were prisoners! I turned around, and looked at my companions. The grave Winnetou showed his splendid ivory teeth; Fred made a face as if he had tasted sugar and alum, and I laughed loud and heartily over this neat trick. "The little monkey thinks we are thieves," exclaimed Fred.

A big signal horn sounded to call the men, and opening one of the little port hole windows I counted sixteen of them gathered around the paymaster, apparently receiving instructions.

"The execution is about to begin," I remarked. "They've got their guns. What shall we do?"

"Light a cigar," replied Fred, suiting the action to the word.

Soon the door opened cautiously, and the paymaster's thin voice called from without: "Don't shoot, you rascals, or we'll shoot you." then he retreated behind a large cask, and from this fortress demanded more confidently: "Who are you?"

"You donkey!" laughed Walker. "First you call us rascals, and then you ask who we are. Come out from behind your cask, and we'll talk to you."

"Not much! What did you come here for?"

"To warn you."

"Warn us! Of what?"

"Of the Ogellallah Sioux and the white train wreckers who are coming to attack Echo Canyon."

"Ridiculous! You're a train wrecker yourself more likely."

I had had enough of this, so I pulled the grimmest face I could, threw my gun over my shoulder, took a revolver in each hand, and marched to the door, followed by Winnetou and Walker. One glance at this demonstration was enough to send Mr. Ohlers completely out of sight behind his cask, and only the end of his gun, sticking up like a grave stone, showed where the valiant leader lay. As to the workmen they respectfully made way for us to pass. These were the people who were to resist the Sioux and the white desperadoes! It was a pleasant prospect for the morrow!

"You see we could shoot you, but we don't," I said to the workmen. "Bring out that brave paymaster of yours for us to talk to, unless he prefers being murdered by the Sioux."

After some urging the little man ventured forth into the daylight, and I told him all I knew.

"I believe you now, sir," he said with trembling voice. "And this gentleman is Mr. Winnetou? Honored, sir, I'm sure." he made a deep bow to the Apache. "And this is Mr. Walker? Delighted to meet you." Another bow. "You think may be the colonel will be back in time?" he continued, addressing me.

"I think so."

"I should be most glad, sir, believe me."

I did believe him as thoroughly as though he had sworn it. However I only asked: "How many has the colonel with him?"

"A hundred. His bravest men."

"So I see. And there are over two hundred coming, with the white men."

"Oh, murder! The only thing to do is to get out of Echo Canyon, and go to the next station."

"Nonsense! What would your employers think of you? What is the largest station near here?"

"Promontory. There are three hundred workmen there."

"Then telegraph them to send you down a hundred well armed men."

He stared at me open mouthed, then sprang up, clapped his hands, and cried: "I never thought of that!"

"Yes, you seem to be a strategic genius. Let them bring provisions and munitions, if you're short. And look here, it must be done as secretly as possible, or the Indian spies will learn they are discovered; telegraph that too. Have you a line to Promontory, and how far is it?"

"Ninety-one miles. Yes, they can run down here."

"Good. Then they ought to be here before daybreak if you telegraph now. Tomorrow night the spies will be here, and in the meantime we will strengthen the wall. Now hurry up. You've three things to do: Telegraph to Promontory; get your place ready for the night, and put your men at work on the wall."

"They shall be done at once, sir," said the little man, his courage completely restored by these arrangements. "And you shall have a supper fit for a king. I'm the cook myself."

Everything was done exactly as we would have it. Our horses had good fodder, and we had such a supper as showed Mr. Ohlers to be more skillful with cooking utensils than with arms. The men worked like giants at building up the wall; they allowed themselves no rest during the night, and when I awoke early in the morning I was surprised at the progress they had made. The train came down from Promontory, bringing the hundred men, and everything necessary in the way of provisions, arms and ammunition. These people took a hand at the work so heartily that it was done by noon. After dinner Winnetou, Fred and I went out of the canyon to look for the spies, first arranging that a mine should be sprung in the canyon if one of us returned with tidings.

We separated; Walker going east, I north, and Winnetou between the two, for we knew the enemy was to come by the north, or east. I climbed the rocky steep, and after three-quarters of an hour came to a place that seemed to be made for my purpose. In the very highest point of the forest stood an oak, with a tall pine beside it. I climbed the latter, and leaned out as far as possible on the strong branches of the oak. For hours I waited in vain, but at last I saw in the north a flock of crows rising from the trees. They did not fly together, nor in any special direction, but straggled along, fluttering in a purposeless way over the trees, into which they settled again one by one. Evidently they had been startled. In a short time I saw another similar flock farther along, and another; the crows were afraid of something coming through the woods from the north. I came down as quickly as I could, and went stealthily in that direction, carefully concealing my tracks. Thus I reached an almost impenetrable thicket of shrubs, into which I forced myself, and laid down to wait.

In a short time one, two, three, four, five, six Indians came one by one, sliding past my hiding-place like shadows. Their feet did not stir the broken twigs lying about. They were the spies, and wore their war paint. As soon as they had passed I hastened back by a shorter way, knowing they must go out of their way for some distance before they would dare go forward. I noticed at once that new men were standing about, but my attention was called from them by Winnetou, whom to my surprise I saw coming in.

"My red brother comes at the same time as I; did he see anything?" I asked.

"Winnetou comes because it is not necessary to wait longer," he replied. "My brother Jack has seen the spies."

"How did Winnetou know that?"

"Winnetou sat in a tree, and took his glass in his hand. Far in the north he saw another tall tree. That was my brother's direction, and since my brother is wise, Winnetou knew he would be in that tree. Then after a time Winnetou saw many specks in the sky; they were birds flying before the spies. My brother must also notice this, and watch the spies, so the Apache chief came back to the camp where the spies will be." this is an instance of the keen sight, and judgment of this Indian.

Just as we entered the camp a man came forward whom we had not seen before.

"Ah, Mr. Hildreth, you have come back from your search?" he asked. "My men saw you coming down the rocks and called me. You know my name already; I am Colonel Rudge, and we owe you profound gratitude."

"There will be time for that, Colonel," I said. "The first thing now is to fire the mine to recall my comrade. Will you give the order for the men to conceal themselves? The spies will be here in a quarter of an hour."

"It shall be done. Go inside yourself, and I'll be back shortly."

A moment later the explosion echoed, so loud that Walker must have heard it. Then the men withdrew into the buildings, so that only a few people were about, all apparently occupied with their ordinary work.

Colonel Rudge was not gone long. When he came in he said immediately: "Tell me how we can show our gratitude to you and your comrades?"

"By saying nothing about it," I answered.

"Well, I hope to find a better way than that some day. When do you think our welcome guests will arrive?"

"They will attack us tomorrow night."

"Then we've time to get acquainted," he laughed. "Come, bring your red friend into my place; you shall be my most honored guests."

He took Winnetou and me to the other stone building which was divided into more apartments. One was his own, which was large enough to accommodate us also. Colonel Rudge had good nerve, and I saw he did not dread the fight that was coming. We felt confidence in one another at once, and Winnetou too, whose name had long been known to the colonel, seemed to like him.

"Come, gentlemen; we'll break the neck of a good bottle, since we can't break our foes' necks just now, and we'll have a pleasant evening," he said after Fred had joined us, and so we did, for there was nothing more to be done.

The night passed peacefully, as did the next day. It was new moon, and perfectly dark in the ravine till the stars came out, which gave light enough to see the broad circle of the wall around us. As the Indians would attack between midnight and dawn, we placed only the necessary sentinels on guard, and the rest lay around in the grass. It was but a brief rest, and as midnight approached the sleepers arose, seized their weapons, and took their appointed places at the windows.

I stood at the door with my Henry rifle in my hand. We had divided our force into four parts, one on each side, two hundred and ten men strong, while thirty were appointed to guard the horses.

The moments seemed to creep; it almost seemed that our fear had been groundless, but hark! Something sounded like a stone falling on the railroad track. Then I heard a rustle, which an unaccustomed ear would have taken for the sighing of the softest breeze. They were coming! "Attention!" I whispered to the man next to me. He passed the word on around the circle. At last ghostly shadows flitted through the darkness, now to left, now to right, without the faintest sound. The shadows drew nearer. They were now only fifteen, twelve, ten, eight, six feet from the wall. Then a loud, sonorous voice rang through the night. *"Selkhi Ogellallah. Ntsage sisi Winnetou, natan Apaches. Shne ko.* [Death to the Ogellallah! Here stands Winnetou, the chief of the Apaches. Fire!]" he raised his silver studded rifle, and its flash lighted all the camp. At the same moment two hundred shots rattled. I had not fired; I waited to see the effect of the salvo, which fell sudden, deadly, like a judgment of heaven on the foe.

For a moment the most profound stillness reigned; then a horrible howl arose which pierced the nerves, and shattered the bones. The unexpectedness of our defense had deprived the savages of breath, but now a din arose as if a thousand demons had broken loose in the valley.

"Once more: Fire!" commanded Rudge, whose voice could be heard above the tumult. A second salvo rattled, and then Rudge cried: "Forward with your tomahawks." I n an instant the men were over the walls; even the frightened ones as bold as lions now.

I remained at my post. All around raged a battle which could not continue long, for the ranks of the enemy had been so frightfully thinned that they could only save themselves by flight.

At last it was over; the wounded lay on the ground; many fires burned outside the wall, and one could see by their light the awful harvest death had garnered in so short a time. I could not look at it, but went away to the colonel's quarters, and sat down alone.

Hardly had I done so when Winnetou entered. I looked up in surprise. "My red brother comes?" I asked. "Where are the scalps of his foes, the Ogellallah Sioux?"

"Winnetou will never take a scalp again," he answered. "Since he has heard the music come down the hillside he will kill his enemy, but leave him his scalp. How!"

At this moment Walker rushed in excitedly. "Jack, Winnetou, come!" he cried. "We have captured Dawson, the leader of the outlaws, and only eighty of the enemy has escaped. But Dawson says they are gone to attack Helldorf Settlement."

"Oh, Lord help us, if that is true!" I cried, as Winnetou and I sprang to our feet.

"It is true; he is triumphing in it. We spoiled their game here, but he says it was arranged that they were to fall back on Helldorf Settlement after they had finished this place up, and not a stone will be left."

"Come!" said Winnetou briefly.

We found the colonel. "Lend us men," I said. "We must do what can be done for those good people."

"I can't lend you men," he said.

"Then how do you expect to face God on the day of judgment?" I asked angrily.

"Listen, my dear fellow," said Colonel Rudge gently. "I can't desert my post; I can't order my men to go with you, but what I can do I will do gladly. You may speak to my men, and if any will leave their work and go with you they shall do so. And you shall have horses, weapons and ammunition, provided you will return them."

"Thank you, Colonel; I am sure you can do no more. Pardon me that I spoke hastily."

Two hours later Winnetou, Walker and I, at the head of forty well-armed men, were tearing back to rescue Helldorf Settlement, which we had left so peaceful but a short time before.

CHAPTER XV

MY BRAVE WINNETOU

WE rode furiously, not resting even during the night. In the entire ride I doubt that there were a hundred words spoken. Winnetou never spoke at all, but in his eyes glowed a fire that said more than any words. It was the second noon when we stopped our sweating horses on the edge of the valley in which Helldorf Settlement had stood. We saw at the first glance that Dawson had spoken the truth, and we had come too late. The entire settlement was a smoking wreck.

Winnetou pointed to the hill. "The Son of the good Manitou is gone. I will rend these wolves of Ogellallahs."

It was true; the chapel had been burned, and the crucifix cast down.

We galloped into the valley, and dismounted. We could not discover a trace of a living being, and though we searched the smoking ruins we found no human remains, which was a great consolation.

Winnetou had gone at once to the site of the chapel, and now returned with the bell in his hand. "The Apache chief has found the voice on the hill," he said. "He will bury it here till he returns victorious."

"There isn't a moment to lose," I cried. "The prisoners have been carried away. We must not delay, but must follow the trail while we can see. When it is dark we will rest, but now let us hasten after them."

With these words I remounted poor Swallow, and we started again, Winnetou leading, his keen eye fastened on the trail. He might die, but he would never turn from this path, such wrath filled him, and filled us all. We were forty against eighty men, but in such a cause one does not stop to count numbers.

We had still three good hours of daylight, and made such distance in them that we were delighted with our horses' extraordinary endurance, and allowed them their well-earned rest. For the first two days we did not gain on our foes, for we dared not press our horses beyond their strength.

"Time flies," said Walker, "and we shall be too late."

"We shall not be too late," I replied. "The prisoners are reserved for torture, and that will not be until the Ogellallah have reached their village."

"And where is that?"

"The villages of the Ogellallah are now beyond Quackingasp Ridge," replied Winnetou, "and we shall not overtake these robbers much short of there."

We passed a point where the force had divided, but, though there were two trails, we distinguished the right one by little drops of blood which had fallen along the way. At a certain spot we saw that the Indians had gone on very slowly, leading their horses. This was strange, and I was considering it, when suddenly Winnetou reined up, looked far ahead, and made a gesture as though he recollected something.

"Ugh!" he cried. "The pit of the hill which the pale-faces call Hancock!"

"What about it?" I asked.

"Now Winnetou knows all. The Sioux sacrifice their prisoners to the Great Spirit in this pit. These Ogellallah have divided; the greater part to call together the scattered hands of their tribe, while the signaler brings the prisoners to the pit. They have been bound on the horses, and the Ogellallah run beside them."

"How far is this mountain from here?"

"My brothers will reach it this evening."

"Impossible! Hancock Mountain is between the Yellowstone and Snake rivers."

"My white brother must remember there are two Hancock mountains. Winnetou knows the right one, and its pit. He and his father once made a compact in this pit with the Ogellallah Sioux, which they broke. My brothers will leave the trail, and trust to the Apache chief."

He spurred his horse, and sprang forward at a gallop; evidently he knew exactly what he was going to do, and we rode after him. We went through valleys and ravines for a time, till suddenly the mountain rose before us, and a grassy plain spread out at our feet.

"That is J-akown akono, the prairie of blood, in the speech of the Tchua," called Winnetou without pausing in his ride.

So that was the horrible bloody prairie of which I had heard so much! Here the united tribes of the Dakotas had brought their prisoners, set them free, and hunted them to death. Here thousands of innocent victims had died at the stake, in the fire, by the knife, and living burial. No Indian or white man wandered here, and we rode over this accursed plain as carelessly as if we were in a peaceful meadow. Only Winnetou could have been our leader. Our horses began to droop. A single hill rose before us, and we let our poor beasts rest in the woods at its foot.

"That is Hancock Mountain," said Winnetou.

"And is the pit here?" I asked.

"Yes; on the other side of the mountain. In an hour my brother will see it. He will follow me, but leave his gun behind."

"Only I?"

"Yes. This is the place of death; only a strong man can bear it. Our brothers may hide under the trees, and wait."

The mountain at whose foot we found ourselves was of volcanic origin, and perhaps three miles broad. I laid aside all my weapons except my knife, and followed Winnetou up its western side. We mounted in short spiral curves; it was a very difficult path, and my guide bent backward cautiously, as if he feared a foe behind each shrub. It took an hour for us to gain the top.

"My brother must be still, still," he whispered as he lay down on his stomach, and slid forward between two bushes. I followed, and almost fell back with horror, for scarcely had I thrust my head between the bushes than I saw directly before me the funnel-shaped, steep abyss of a crater fully a hundred and fifty feet deep, the edge of which I could reach with my hand. At the bottom was a plain about fifty feet in diameter, and there lay the people of Helldorf Settlement whom we sought, bound hand and foot, and guarded by a large Ogellallah watch. I conquered my horror, and counted our friends; none was missing. I looked over each foot of this extinct crater, to see if there was any way of getting into it. Yes, it might be done, if one were cunning, and had a stout rope, and could get the guards away. There were several jutting rocks which could be used as holding, or resting points. Winnetou crept back, and I did the same.

"We can get down there," I said. "We have lassos, and the railroad men are well supplied with ropes."

Winnetou nodded, and we began the descent. The sun dropped behind the mountain as we reached its foot, and we began our preparations. All our ropes were tied together in one long rope, and Winnetou picked out twenty of the most experienced men for the enterprise; the others were to watch the horses. We arranged that three-quarters of an hour after we started two of the men were to jump on their horses, and ride around the mountain toward the east, kindle a fire, and then return. This fire was to distract the attention of the Indian guards from us to that part of the prairie.

The sun had set, and the west was tinted with crimson, fading to purple, and dying away into the gray of evening. Winnetou had left his place among us. He seemed to be quite unlike his usual self in the last hour. The steady light of his eye had given way to a peculiar restless sparkle, and on his brow, always smooth and calm, a frown had gathered, indicating unusual gravity of thought, or anxiety disturbing the equilibrium of his soul at which I had so often wondered. It was not only my right, but my duty to inquire into this, and I rose up, and followed him. He stood at the edge of the woods, leaning against a tree, his eyes fixed on the west and the clouds piled on the horizon, their edges golden with the day's last splendor. Although I came softly, and he was sunk in thought, he not only heard my step, but recognized it. Without turning toward me he said: "My brother Jack comes to look for his friend. He is right, for in a little while he will see him no more."

I laid my hand on his shoulder, and said: "Are there shadows over the spirit of my brother Winnetou? He must drive them away."

He raised his hand, and pointed to the west. "There burns the flame of life; it is gone, and darkness comes. Can you drive away the shadows that fall there?"

"No, but the light comes again in the morning, and a new day breaks."

"For Hancock Mountain a new day will begin, but not for Winnetou. His sun will set, as this one has set, and will never rise again. The next dawn will smile at him on the other side of those clouds."

"That is a presentiment of death which my dearest brother Winnetou must not yield to. To-night will be dangerous for us, but how often has death stretched out his hand for us, and we escaped him! Throw off the weight that oppresses you. It is caused by the mental and bodily exertions of the last few days."

"No; Winnetou's exertions do not master him, and no weariness can rob him of the serenity of his soul. My brother Old Shatterhand knows me, and knows that I have thirsted for the waters of knowledge and learning, and you have poured them out for me, and I have drunk of them in deep draughts. I have learned much, more than any of my brethren, but I have remained a red man. The whites are like the domestic beasts whose instinct has almost disappeared, but the Indian is the wild beast, who has not only kept his sharp senses, but hears with his soul. The red man knows exactly when death comes near him; he does not suspect it, but feels its coming, and crouches in the deepest thicket of the wood to die calmly and alone. This presentiment, this feeling which never deceives has come to Winnetou now.

I drew him to me, and said: "And yet it deceives you. Have you ever had this feeling before?"

"No!'

"Then how can you recognize it for the presentiment of death?"

"It is so plain, so plain. It tells me that Winnetou will die with a bullet in the breast, for only a bullet can reach me; the Apache chief could defend himself against a knife, or a tomahawk. My brother may believe me; I go to the Happy --"

He stopped. "To the Happy Hunting Grounds," he would have said, according to Indian belief. What prevented him finishing that sentence? I knew; he had been a Christian in heart since our talk at Helldorf Settlement.

He threw his arm around me, and corrected his half finished words. "I go today where the Son of the good Manitou has gone to prepare our dwelling in His Father's house, and where some day my brother Jack will follow. There we shall meet again, and there will be no difference between the white and red children of the Father who loves them both with the same love. There will be eternal peace; no more murder; no more crushing out of men who were good, and came to the whites peacefully and confidently, yet were destroyed. Then the good Manitou will hold the scales of the world to judge the deeds of the white and red, and the innocent blood which has been shed. But Winnetou will stand by and beg for mercy for the murderers of his nation, his brothers."

He pressed me to him, and was silent. I was profoundly moved, and an inward voice whispered to me: "His instinct has never deceived him; perhaps this time too it speaks the truth." nevertheless I said: "My brother Winnetou considers himself stronger than he is. He is the mightiest warrior of his race, but he is only a man. I have never seen him tired, but the last few nights and days have been too much for us all. Exhaustion prostrates the soul, weakens our self-confidence, and gloomy thoughts come, which disappear when we are rested. My brother should rest. Stay with the men whom we leave here to guard the horses."

He shook his head slowly: "My brother Jack does not say that in earnest."

"Yes, I do! I have seen the crater, and measured it exactly with my eye; I can lead the attack alone."

"And I not be there?" he asked, a proud light in his eyes.

"You have done enough; rest!"

"Have you not done enough too, even more than I, and all the rest? I will not stay behind."

"Not even if I beg you to as a sacrifice for my sake?"

"Not even then. Shall it be said that Winnetou, the chief of the Apaches, feared death?"

"No man would dare say it."

"And if all the rest were silent, and did not count me a coward, one would do so, and his reproach would redden my cheeks with shame."

"And that is --?"

"I myself. I would forever cry in the ear of that Winnetou who rested while his brother Jack fought, that he should be among the cowards, and was no longer worthy to call himself a warrior, a chief of his brave people. No, no; do not ask me to stay behind."

I could say no more; it would be better for Winnetou to die than to live with such a feeling.

After a short pause he continued: "We have often faced death, and my brother was prepared for it, and wrote in a little book what should be done if he fell in combat. I was to take the book and read it, and do as it said. That is called a will by the pale-faces. Winnetou has also made a will, though he has not spoken of it. Today when he feels the approach of death he must do so. Will you carry it out?"

"Yes. I hope, I know, your presentiment will not be fulfilled; you will see many, many suns arise, but if you die it shall be my most sacred duty to do whatever you ask of me."

"Even if it were hard, very hard, and included many dangers?"

"Winnetou does not ask that seriously. Send me to death, and I will go."

"I know it, Jack. You would spring in the open abyss for me. You will do what I ask of you; you alone can do it. When I am dead seek my father's grave. When you are at its foot, exactly on the west side, you will find buried in the ground the will of Winnetou, who will be no longer with you. I have explained my wishes there, and you will fulfill them."

"My word is like an oath," I assured him with tears in my eyes. "No danger, however great, shall prevent me doing what you have written there."

"I thank you. And now we are ready. The time to attack has come. I shall not live beyond this combat. Let us say good-by, my dear, dear Jack. May the good Manitou repay you for having been so much, so much to me. My heart feels more than I can say in words. Let us not weep, for we are men. Bury me in the Gros Ventre hills, on my horse, with all my weapons, and my father's silver-studded rifle, that it may not fall into other hands. And then when you go back to the people in the East, of whom none will love you as I love you, think sometimes of your friend and brother Winnetou, who blesses you, for you have been a blessing to him."

He, the Indian, laid his hands on my head. He repressed a sob with difficulty, and as I held him to me, I wept outright.

"Winnetou, my Winnetou," I cried, "it is only a presentiment, a shadow that passes over you. You must stay with me; you can't leave me."

"I go away," he answered softly, but clearly; then he released himself from my arms, and turned back to the camp. As I followed him I tried in vain to find a means to keep him from the fight, but there was none. What would I have given, and what would I give today, had I been able to?

I was utterly unarmed, and in spite of his self control, I heard his voice tremble as he called to the men: "It is now quite dark; let us go. My brothers may follow me and Old Shatterhand."

We climbed the mountain behind one another, by the way Winnetou and I had previously gone up. The steep ascent was even more difficult in the darkness, and it took more than an hour for us to reach the edge of the crater. Looking over we saw a great fire burning, and by its light we saw the prisoners and their guards. Not a sound escaped us. We fastened our rope to a crag, and waited for the fire on the prairie. It was not long before three, four, and five fires which looked like camp fires blazed up in the east. We looked and listened down the crater. We were not mistaken in the anticipated effect, for soon an Indian appeared through a fissure from the other side of the crater, spoke to one of the guards, who arose and went with him through the cleft to observe the fires. Now was our time. I seized the swinging rope to be the first to go down, but Winnetou took it out of my hand.

"The chief of the Apaches is the leader," he said. "My brother comes behind me."

Winnetou swung out, I after him, Fred last. We had arranged to trust only four at a time on the rope, which fortunately held. Of course as we slid down we displaced a great many rocks, which rolled into the crater. One of them must have struck a child, for it began to cry, and the head of an Indian appeared in the fire-lighted fissure. He heard the stones, looked up, and gave a cry of warning.

"Forward, Winnetou or all is lost," I cried.

The men above saw what had happened, and slackened the rope. A half minute later we should have reached the bottom, but at that instant a shot rang out from the cleft.

Winnetou fell to the ground. I stood still in horror." Winnetou, my friend, are you wounded?" I cried.

"Winnetou dies," he answered.

A mad fury possessed me. "Winnetou is dying," I cried to Walker. "Forward." I did not take time to snatch my rifle from my shoulder, or draw a knife or revolver. With raised fist I threw myself on the five Indians who had already come through the cleft. The foremost of them was the chief, whom I recognized instantly. "Down, Ko-itse," I cried. A blow felled him like a log. The Indian behind him had raised his tomahawk to strike me, but the firelight fell on my face, and he dropped the tomahawk in fright.

"Ka-ut-skamasti, Shatterhand!" he cried.

"Yes; here is Old Shatterhand; down with you," I cried. I did not know myself. The second blow knocked this man down.

"Ka-ut-skamasti," cried the Indians.

I received a knife wound in the shoulder, but scarcely felt it. Two of the Indians fell before Fred's shots, and I knocked down a third. Meanwhile more of our men had come down the rope, and I could leave the Indians to them. I turned back to Winnetou, and knelt beside him.

"Where is my brother wounded?" I asked.

"Here, in the breast," he answered softly, laying his left hand on the right side of his breast, reddened by his blood.

I drew my knife, and cut the blanket that wound around him. Yes; the bullet had entered the lung. A pain gripped my heart such as I had never felt in my happy young life.

"My friend will lay me on his bosom that I may see the fight," he whispered.

I did so, and he saw that as fast as the Indians came through the fissure they were shot down. By degrees all our men had descended the rope, the prisoners were freed, and raised a shout of joy and gratitude.

I saw nothing but my dying friend, whose wound had ceased to bleed, and I knew this meant that he was bleeding inwardly.

"Has my brother any wish?" I asked.

He had closed his eyes, and did not reply. I held his head on my arm, and hung over him motionless, my eyes fastened on the bronze features and closed lids of the Apache. At last Walker, who was wounded, came to me and said: "They are all dead."

"This one will also die," I replied. "All the others are nothing beside him."

Still Winnetou laid still. The railroad men and the settlers formed a silent circle around us.

At last Winnetou opened his eyes. "Has my dear brother any wish?" I repeated.

He nodded. "My brother Jack will lead the men to the Gros Ventre mountains. They will find such stones as they seek; they deserve them."

"What more, Winnetou?"

"My brother, do not forget the Apache. He will pray for him to the great, good Manitou. Are these people able to climb with their wounded limbs?"

"Yes," I said, though I saw how the settlers' hands and feet had been torn.

"Winnetou begs them to sing the song to the Queen of Heaven."

They had heard what he said, and without waiting started at once up a rocky point, just above Winnetou's head. His eyes followed them, then closed. He grasped both my hands, and listened as they sang:

> "Now the light of day is fading,
> Night enfolds us, still and gray;
> Would that grief, our poor hearts lading,
> Might with daylight steal away.
> Mary, Mother, interceding,
> Lay our sighs before God's feet,
> While thy children humbly pleading,
> From your loving hearts repeat:
> *Ave Maria.*"

As they began the second stanza he opened his eyes, and raised them, with a gentle, smiling look to the stars. "Jack, are not these the words of death?"

Sobbing, I bowed my head, and they sang:

> "Now the last ray disappearing,
> Still and gray falls death's dark night,
> And the Soul, its summons hearing,
> Spreads its wings to take its flight.
> Mary, at this hour defending,
> In thy hands our prayer we lay
> Help us when our life is ending;
> Wake us to eternal day:
> *Ave Maria.*"

As the last note died away he tried to speak, but could not. I brought my ear close to his lips, and in my hand I held the canteen of water I had carried over my shoulder. With the last effort of his failing strength Winnetou whispered: "Jack, I believe in the Savior. Winnetou is a Christian. Goodbye."

I poured the water on his head thrice. "Winnetou, I baptize thee, in the name of the Father, and of the Son, and of the Holy Ghost," I said.

A convulsive tremor passed through his body; a stream of blood burst from his lips; his hands slipped from mine; his limbs straightened. My brother, doubly my brother in that moment, was dead.

I passed the night holding him in my arms as he had died, in speechless, tearless grief. Were it possible, how gladly would I have divided my remaining years with him!

We buried Winnetou in the spot he had chosen, with Christian prayers, and with the honor due so great a chief. He sits on his horse with all his weapons around him, in the bosom of the Gros Ventre hills. But no scalps of enemies wave on his grave, as are usual on the grave of a chief, but a cross speaks of peace.

The stones he promised to be found in this place were found abundantly, and a new Helldorf Settlement was made near his grave. Here we brought the bell of the old settlement which Winnetou had buried, and it swings in the belfry of the new chapel. When its voice recalls the Angelus hour to the settlers, they think of my brave Winnetou, who died to save them, and know his dying prayer is granted:

> "Wake us to eternal day.
> *Ave Maria.*"

CHAPTER XVI

BACK TO NUGGET MOUNTAIN

FOR two weeks I lingered by Winnetou's grave. I was benumbed at first, and saw the good people working on the new Helldorf Settlement, and listened to their voices as in a dream, too listless and heavy-hearted to be of any use, or feel any interest in what went on around me.

The kindly settlers tried to arouse me from my lethargy of sorrow sufficiently to be of some use in planning the little settlement for which Winnetou died. Helping others helped me, as it does every one, and two weeks after Winnetou had been laid to rest in the heart of the mountain I realized that I must no longer dally by his grave. My friend's last request called me for its fulfillment.. I must go back to Rio Pecos to tell his people how he died, and then to Nugget Mountain to find the paper which should speak his last words to me.

I parted from the good settlers with hearty affection and regret on both sides, and leaving Walker with them till he should be quite recovered, and they well established, mounted on Swallow, who was thoroughly rested, and set out on my long ride.

I was so impatient to get Winnetou's letter that I went straight to Nugget Mountain, leaving Rio Pecos till afterward. The way was dangerous, but I rode cautiously, and came safely through the Sioux country, and then the Kiowas', and at last, one night toward sunset, saw once more Nugget Mountain rising before me. I laid at its foot till dawn, and then with a heavy heart, climbed the mountain which I had last seen when Winnetou and I descended it together.

The tombs were there undisturbed. The stone mound beneath which Intschu-Tschuna rested on his horse, with his weapons around him, as became a brave warrior, and beside it the stone pyramid, with the branches of the tree waving from its apex, beneath which Nscho-Tschi sat sleeping her last sleep. And now in the heart of the Wyoming mountains, Winnetou was at rest.

I looked around to be sure that I was alone, and with my knife cut out a piece of turf in the spot Winnetou had designated, and began digging. I spread my coat on the ground, and piled on it the dirt I took out to fill in the hole again afterward. I worked with feverish haste, stopping at intervals to listen for a step or a voice. The hole grew deeper and deeper, and at last my knife struck a stone, which I took out, and then a second one which lay under it, and then I saw a square space, lined with stone, and perfectly dry. At the bottom was a leather wrapped package: the will of my brother Winnetou. The next moment I had thrust it in my pocket, and was hastily filling in the hole. This went much faster than the digging, for I had only to shake back the dirt in my coat, pound it down, replace the piece of sod I had cut out, and no one could tell that a hole had been dug there.

Thank heaven! I had succeeded! I listened; there was not the slightest sound. I opened the leather, which was held together with nails, and inside was a second cover, which Winnetou had tied together with deer tendons. I cut them, and saw several leaves of closely written paper. For Winnetou could write; Kleki-Petrah, his white teacher, had taught him this, as well as so much else. He had never had much occasion to use this accomplishment, and he wrote the careful, stiff hand of a school-boy trying to follow his copybook faithfully, but he wrote very plainly. How long, how very long he must have worked over this last message to me!

My eyes filled with tears; I dried them, and read: "My dear good brother: You live, and Winnetou, who loved you, is dead. But his soul is with you; you hold it in your hand, for it is written on these pages. Let the words rest in your heart. You shall learn the last wish of your red brother, and read many words from him which you will never forget, but first I will say to you what is necessary to say. Here you have not the only will of Winnetou, for it lives in the souls of his red warriors. This is for you alone. You will see a great deal of gold, and will do with it what my spirit tells you. It lies hidden in Nugget-tsil - -" I had read to this point when I heard a voice behind me saying: "Good day, Mr. Shatterhand. Are you perfecting yourself in the spelling-book?" I looked up. Santer stood by me smiling derisively.

The shock of seeing him, of raising my eyes from Winnetou's last words, as I sat by his father's grave, to the face of his murderer, was indescribable, and at the same instant I recognized the fact that I had been guilty of the greatest stupidity of my life. I had laid aside all my weapons, even my belt with my knife and revolver, because they were in my way as I bent down to dig, and had left them ten feet behind me. And now here was Santer!

He laughed as he saw my futile movement for my weapons. "Not a step from that spot; not a movement after your weapons, or I'll shoot instantly. I'm in deadly earnest," he said.

His sudden appearance so stunned me, that I stared at him without moving. "At last I've got you," he continued. "Do you see my finger on the trigger? The least movement, and I'll blaze away into your brains. You did not expect to meet me here, eh?"

"No," I answered quietly.

"Well, you'll be glad to hear how it came about. I've been to tell Tangua that the Apache cur, your friend, was at last put an end to, for I knew how glad he'd be to hear it. And then I came here with three men that I've got together to look for that gold which I know is somewhere in this mountain. You see, I am frank with you, because you're in my power, and because I know it drives you mad to hear that I shall get your beloved redskin's treasure at last. What is that paper you have in your hand?"

"A tailor's bill," I said.

"Yes, of course. Don't be funny. I tell you, you dog, it's all up with you."

"Or with you; it's one of the two, that's certain."

"Impudent mongrel that you are! You snarl like a cur to the last. But that's all the good it will do; I repeat: It's all up with you, and that paper in your hand will give the information we want."

"Come get it then."

"I'll have it fast enough, but I won't take any risks with such a dangerous fellow as you are. Come here, and bind him, Gates." a t these words three men came out from behind the trees with thongs in their hands.

"Drop that paper, and hold out your hands to him," ordered Santer.

I obediently dropped the paper.

"Now your hands." I held them out to Gates with apparent submission, but in such a way that he had to get between me and Santer to tie them.

"Stand aside; you're in the way of my gun," he shouted. Before Gates could move I had seized him around the waist, lifted him, and hurled him against Santer, who sprang aside, but too late. He was knocked down, and his gun dropped from his hand. In an instant I was kneeling on him. A blow from my fist knocked him senseless. Then I arose, and shouted to the others: "That was proof that I am Shatterhand. Drop your weapons, or I'll shoot; I too am in earnest."

I had taken Santer's revolver from his belt, and aimed at the three men. "Go and sit down on the grave of the chief's daughter," I said, choosing this place because it was farthest from the weapons, and they obeyed promptly.

"This is awful," moaned Gates, rubbing his sides. "Perfectly horrible. I flew through the air like a ball. I'm sure I'm broken somewhere."

"It's your own fault; take care nothing worse happens to you. Now, give me those thongs."

He produced them, and I bound Santer's feet together, and his arms behind his back. It was not long before he opened his eyes, and saw his comrades sitting on the Indian girl's grave. I was fastening my belt. "Have you blabbed?" he asked Gates at once.

"No," replied Gates.

"What should he blab about?" I demanded.

"Nothing."

"See here, speak up, or I'll open your mouth. Now then?"

"About the gold," Santer answered with apparent reluctance.

"Is that true; did he mean nothing else?" I asked Gates. "That's all," he replied. "I don't believe you; your face and manner show you are trying to deceive. Was Santer alone when he came up here, except for you?"

"Yes."

"Well, this is the end of your gold, for Santer is my prisoner, and must pay for his crimes with his life."

Santer laughed scornfully as I said this, and I turned to him. "You will feel less like laughing a little later. What is to prevent me putting a bullet through your head?"

"Yourself. Everybody knows Old Shatterhand is afraid to kill a man."

"I certainly am no murderer, but you have deserved death again and again. I am a Christian, and do not seek revenge, but you must be punished."

"Don't make beautiful speeches. It's all the same thing whether you call it punishment or revenge, so don't show off with your Christianity."

"I have no idea of taking your life, but I will send you to the nearest fort, and deliver you over to justice."

"Really? Do you know I venture to doubt that? I think you'll be carried off yourself, and as I'm not such a pious saint as you it won't occur to me to renounce my revenge. There they are already, see They're coming." he uttered these words triumphantly, and with good reason, for a howl arose on all sides at once, and the Kiowas in full war-paint burst upon me. Gates had lied to me; Santer had not been alone in coming here, but had brought the Kiowas with him to Nugget Mountain to celebrate the death of Winnetou by his father's grave.

The attack was so sudden that I had not time to think, and drew my revolver, but as I saw myself surrounded by sixty warriors I put it back in my belt. Flight was impossible, and resistance useless. I drew back from the hands stretched out to seize me, and cried in a loud voice: "Old Shatterhand yields himself a prisoner to the Kiowas. Is the young chief here? To Pida, but to him only, I will freely give myself up."

"Freely!" mocked Santer." this fellow who calls himself Old Shatterhand so loftily, needn't talk about doing it freely. He has to give himself up or be taken by force. Seize him." he took care not to seize me himself, however, though the Indians had liberated him. The Kiowas obeyed him, and crowded around me, but used no weapon because they wanted to take me alive. I defended myself with all my might, and knocked down several, but of course I could not have withstood such numbers, if Pida had not appeared and cried: "Stop! Let him alone; he gives himself up to me, and there is no need of attacking him."

Santer cried out angrily: "Why should he be spared? Let him have as many blows as there are arms to give them. Take him; I command it."

The young chief stepped up to him, and said with a gesture that did not signify much respect for him: "You dare to give commands here? Do you know who leads these warriors?"

"You."

"And who are you?"

"The Kiowas' friend, whose will it is to be hoped they will respect."

"A friend? Who says that?"

"Your father."

"That is not true. Tangua, the Kiowa chief, never used that word toward you. You are nothing but a paleface whom we merely tolerate among us." then turning to me, Pida said: "Old Shatterhand will be my prisoner. Will he freely give me what he has with him?"

"Yes."

"And let himself be bound?"

"Yes."

"Then give me your weapons."

I was pleased that he asked this of me, for it showed he feared me. I gave him the revolver and knife, but the Henry rifle and bear-killer Santer picked up, and appropriated to himself.

"Put those down," said Pida, turning on him. "Why do you take my guns?"

"Not such; they're mine."

Pida raised his hand threateningly. "Lay them down this moment."

"I will not."

"Bind him again."

As Santer saw the hands extended to seize him, he threw down the weapons, saying contemptuously: "Here they are, but you won't keep them; I'll complain to Tangua."

"Do," said Pida, with a scornful look.

Santer came over to me. "You may have the guns," he said, "but I will have everything in his pocket."

He stretched out his hand toward the pocket where I had put Winnetou's letter. "Back," I ordered.

He fell back, frightened by my voice, but rallied instantly, and said: "I will know what you dug up."

"Don't try to take it."

"I certainly will. I know it will make you crazy to have this treasure in my hands, but you'll have to stand it."

He made a dash at me with both hands. Mine were not yet thoroughly bound; with a jerk I freed them, took Santer by the breast with my left hand, and with the right gave him a blow on the head that felled him like an ox.

"Ugh, Ugh, Ugh," cried all the Indians.

"Now bind me again," I said, holding out my hands to them.

"Old Shatterhand tells his name by his acts," said the young chief admiringly. "What is it that this Santer wants from you?"

"A written paper," I answered, not daring to tell him more.

"He called it a treasure."

"Nonsense; he doesn't know what it is. Whose prisoner am I, yours or his?"

"Mine."

"Then why do you allow him to attack and rob me?"

"The red warriors will have only your weapons; they cannot use anything else."

"Is that any reason to give it to this fellow? Is Old Shatterhand a boy that any ragamuffin can empty his pockets? I gave myself up to you, and respect you as a warrior and a chief; don't forget I too am a warrior whose footstool this Santer is only fit to fetch."

The Indians respect pride and courage, even in a foe, and Pida remembered that I had once taken him captive, and treated him kindly. I counted on this, and not in vain, for his eyes were far from unfriendly as he answered: "Old Shatterhand is the bravest of the white warriors, but the one you have knocked down has two tongues, and two faces, and sometimes shows one, and sometimes the other. He shall not touch your pockets."

"I thank you. You are worthy to be a chief, and will be the most renowned of the Kiowas. A noble warrior kills his foe, but does not humble him."

I saw my words made him proud, and the tone was almost compassionate in which he said: "Yes; he kills his foe. Old Shatterhand must die, and not only die, but be tortured."

"Torture me, and kill me; you shall not hear a groan from my lips, but keep this beast away from me."

Santer recovered consciousness at this moment, and springing to his feet, darted toward me, raging like a wild beast. He drew his pistol, and cried: "You cur, your last hour has come."

The Indian next to him knocked up his hand, and the shot whizzed by harmlessly.

"Why do you stop me?" he roared, turning on the Indian fiercely. "I can do what I will, I tell you."

"No; you cannot do what you will," said Pida, going up to him, and taking hold of his arm warningly. "Old Shatterhand belongs to me; his life is mine; no one else can take it. You did my father a service, for which we allow you to be with us; don't presume on it. I tell you if you touch Old Shatterhand you shall die by my hand."

"Then what are you going to do with him?" asked Santer, sullenly.

"Take him to our village, where he will die."

"You are very foolish. He has been taken prisoner often, and he will escape again if you do not kill him here, where his friends, and your enemies are buried."

"Silence! Pida is not foolish. Nor will he escape. He shall be watched so that flight is impossible, but he shall be treated as such a renowned warrior should be."

"Confound it! Treated like a renowned warrior! Why don't you twine garlands around him, and hang orders on his breast?"

"Pida does not know what orders and garlands are," said the young chief simply. "But he knows that he will treat Old Shatterhand very differently than we would you, if you were our prisoner. No more words. Go back among my warriors. We will start at once for Salt Fork, and take our prisoner to Tangua, the chief."

CHAPTER XVII

IN THE HANDS OF THE KIOWAS

I WAS taken to the Kiowa village, which looked precisely as it did when I left it, with the case reversed, and Pida my prisoner, instead of I his. I was bound to a strong fir, the significance of which I did not learn till later. This fir was called the death tree, because only those prisoners destined to death by torture were bound to it.

Two armed braves were stationed before me at the right and left as guards, but I was kindly and respectfully treated, and Tangua seemed rather to remember that I had spared him his son, and even his own life, than that I had crippled him.

After I had been fastened to the tree, Pida came to see that my bonds were strong. They were drawn fearfully tight, and the young chief loosened them, saying to the guards: "You must watch him with extraordinary vigilance, but do not hurt him. He is a great chief among the white men, and has never given a red warrior unnecessary pain."

Santer used every art and means to get the paper he had seen me reading into his possession. Tangua would have consented to his having it, but Pida interfered, and prevented the command being given. I was forced, however, to relinquish it to the young chief's keeping, which was the hardest pang I had to endure, and made me desperately anxious fear that by foul means, since fair had failed, Santer would get hold of it.

When Pida made his evening visit to me he said: "Has the white warrior any wish?"

"Yes," I replied, "I want to make a request."

"Tell me it; if I can I will gladly fulfill it."

"I want to warn you of Santer."

"Of him? Beside Pida, the son of the chief Tangua, he is an insect."

"True, but the insect must be guarded against if it will sting. I have heard he dwells beside you?"

"Yes; it is an empty tent."

"Take care he does not come into yours; he mean to."

"I will throw him out."

"What if you were not in your tent when he came?"

"My squaw would be there, and drive him away."

"He is after the speaking paper you took from me."

"He will not get it."

"No; you will never give it to him, I know, but he might steal it."

"Even if he should get into the tent he cannot find it, for it is hidden in my medicine charm, and it is safe."

"I hope so. Would you let me see it once more?"

"You have already seen it, and read it."

"Not all of it."

"Then you shall see it all, but it is growing too dark now. Early in the morning when it is light I will bring it to your."

"I thank you. And now one word more. Santer is not only after the speaking paper, but my weapons. They are famous, and he would like to have them. In whose hands are they now?"

"In mine. The guns I have covered with two blankets, and put under my bed where he will not look for them. They belong to me now. I should like to be your successor in the glory of having a Henry rifle, and so Old Shatterhand can do me a favor."

"I will, certainly, if I can."

"I can shoot with your bear-killer, but not with the Henry rifle. Before you die would you show me how to load and use it?"

"Yes,"

"I thank you. You were not obliged to tell me this secret, and if you did not the rifle would be useless. In return I will see that when your torture begins you have all your heart desires."

He left me, not realizing what a hope this awoke in my heart.

After Pida had gone the women of the village came over to see the white warrior of whom they had heard so much, though the men, and even the lads, were too proud to show curiosity in regard to me, an act of self denial at which I wondered, knowing the nature of a boy, and feeling sure a red one must be very like a white one. Among the maidens was a young girl, standing a little apart from the others. She was not precisely pretty, but she was far from plain, and the steady, earnest, open gaze of her large eyes recalled Nscho-Tschi to me, though there was little resemblance between her and the daughters of the Apaches. I bowed to her pleasantly; she blushed, and walked on, paused to look back at me a moment, and then disappeared in the doorway of one of the larger and finer tents.

"Who was the young daughter of the Kiowas who stood by herself and has just gone away?" I asked my guard.

"That was Kakho-Oto ["Dark Hair"], the daughter of Sus-Homasche ["One Feather"], who, when he was still a boy, won the right to wear a feather in his hair. The squaw of our young chief is her sister."

In a short time Dark Hair came out of the tent; she carried a small clay dish, and walked straight over to the "tree of death."

"My father has allowed me to bring you something to eat; will you take it?" she asked.

"Gladly," I answered, "only I can't use my hands because they are fastened."

"They need not be untied; I will serve you," she said.

She had brought me roasted buffalo meat, cut into small pieces, and carried a knife with which she speared the bits, and put them into my mouth. Old Shatterhand fed by a young Indian girl like a baby! I wanted to laugh, in spite of the gravity of my situation, and I thought my guards had difficulty in keeping sober, but my kind friend was not a self-conscious young white lady, but a simple Indian girl, to whom the situation held nothing funny, and it would never do to smile. So I took my meat with due solemnity and gratitude, and made a hearty supper.

Early in the dawn, before it was light, Pida rode away at the head of a little band to hunt, and I learned that he would not return till noon. I sighed impatiently to think I should have to wait so many hours before I could read Winnetou's letter which Pida had promised to bring me.

An hour passed; then I saw Santer under the tress. He led his saddled horse by the bridle, and carried his gun over his shoulders. He came directly over to me.

"I too am going on the chase, Mr. Shatterhand. I may meet Pida, who is so well disposed toward you, and distrusts me so much." he waited for an answer, but I acted as though I neither saw nor heard him.

"You have grown deaf?"

Again no answer.

"I am awfully sorry, for your sake, and my own.." he put out his hand toward me with insulting affectionateness.

"Keep off, scoundrel," I cried.

"Oh, you can speak, if you can't hear. Pity, dreadful pity; I want to ask you something." he looked me impudently in the face, and his own had a fiendish expression of triumph. "Ha! ha! ha!" he laughed. "What a picture! The renowned Old Shatterhand at the death tree, and the scamp Santer a free man. But there's something better than that to come, much better. Are you going to do with the gold what his spirit told you?"

These words electrified me, for they were from Winnetou's letter.

"Wretch! Where did you learn that?" I demanded. "You have the paper."

"Yes; I have it," he said with triumphant, mocking laughter.

"You have robbed Pida."

"Robbed him! Nonsense! Folly! I have taken what belonged to me; is that stealing? I have the paper, and the whole package."

":Hold him. Catch him; he has robbed Pida," I shouted to the guards.

"Hold me!" he laughed, springing into the saddle. "Not much!"

"Don't let him go: He mustn't get away; he has robbed Pida;" the words stuck in my throat; I could say no more, because I was tearing and pulling to get free.

Santer made off in a gallop and the guards only stared after him with uncomprehending eyes. Winnetou's letter, my brother Winnetou's last will was stolen, and the thief was riding away over the open plain, and no one made a motion to catch him. I was beside myself, and pulled, pulled, pulled with all my might at the thongs that bound my hands to the tree. I did not stop to think they were unbreakable, and that if they were broken I could not move because my feet were tied; I did not feel the pain of their cutting into my flesh; I pulled and pulled, and called and called till I fell forward on the ground. They were broken!

"Ugh, Ugh; he is free!" cried the guards.

"Let me go, let me go; I won't escape. I will only catch Santer. He has robbed your young chief."

My cries had, of course, aroused the whole village. Everybody hastened to hold me, which was easily done, for my feet were still bound, and soon my hands were again tied to the tree.

"Ugh, ugh, ugh!" they cried." broke loose -- no buffalo could have done it. Who could have believed it?" such were the exclamations on all sides, and the Indians seemed rather to admire me than be displeased at the feat.

"Don't stand staring at me," I shrieked. "Didn't you understand what I said? Santer has robbed Pida. Get your horses, quick, and bring him back." no one moved. I was frantic, almost insane with rage, but I could do nothing, absolutely nothing, and my last hope failed when the Indians reported that Tangua had forbidden them to follow Santer because Pida could not read the "speaking paper," and it was of no use to him. So seeing that I was powerless, I forced myself to an outward calm, though I was well-nigh mad to think that Winnetou's long, loving letter, written with such infinite pains, and giving his orders as to the hidden treasure, was in the hands of his father's murderer.

Perhaps three hours passed when I heard a woman's voice call loudly. I had seen without noting that Dark Hair had been going in and out of her tent, and now she and her father came running to where I stood, calling loudly. "Old Shatterhand knows everything; is he also a doctor?"

"Yes," I replied, hoping to be untied and taken to some sick person.

"Can you cure the sick?"

"Yes."

"But not raise the dead?"

"Is there any one dead?"

"Yes; the squaw of the young chief Pida. The medicine-man says she is dead, killed by Santer, who stole the 'speaking paper.' Will Old Shatterhand come to her, and give her back her life?"

"Take me to her."

I was unfastened from the tree, and with long thongs on my hands and feet, was led to Pida's tent, the way to which I was very glad to learn, for my weapons were there. I followed One Feather into the tent, and glanced hastily around. Yes; there they were, my revolver, knife and saddle, and Pida had said the others were under the bed.

"Old Shatterhand may examine the dead, and see if he can make her alive again."

I knelt down, and examined her with my fastened hands. After a time I discovered that her blood still circulated, and I looked up at her father and sister who kept their eyes fastened on me with anxious expectation. "She is dead; no one can awaken her," said the medicine-man.

"Old Shatterhand can," I said.

"Can you? Can you really?" asked One Feather quickly and gladly.

"Wake her, oh, wake her," pleaded Dark Hair, laying her hands on my shoulder.

"Yes, I can, and I will," I repeated. "but if life is to be called back to her, I must be alone with the dead."

"Ugh! Do you know what you ask? Here are your weapons. If you get them, you are free. Promise me not to touch them."

It may be imagined what a struggle this cost me; if I had the knife I could cut my bonds. But no! I would not take advantage of a woman's helplessness for such an end. I saw some little knives that lay on a table, which had been used for some feminine work.

"I promise you," said at last. "You can take them away with you to make sure."

"No; it is not necessary. What Old Shatterhand promises is sure. But that is not enough."

"What more?"

"Promise me not to escape, but to go back to the tree of death, and let yourself be tied."

"I give you my word I will do so."

"Then come away. Old Shatterhand is no liar like Santer; we can trust him."

As soon as they had gone I slipped one of the little knives up my sleeve, then I turned all my attention to the young squaw. I found her head badly swollen from a blow, and as I pressed it she breathed a sigh of pain, opened her eyes, and looked up at me, at first blankly, and then with more consciousness, and at last she whispered: "Old Shatterhand."

"You know me?" I asked.

"Yes."

"Collect yourself; if you sink away again you will die. What has happened?"

My warning that she would die had a good effect. She made an effort, and with my help sat up, laid her hands on her aching head, and said: "I was alone. Santer came in and demanded the medicine. I would not give it to him, and he struck me; I knew no more."

"Is the medicine gone too?"

She looked around, uttered a feeble cry of horror, and said: "It is gone; he has taken it."

The loss of his medicine charm is irreparable to an Indian; Pida would have to ride after Santer, and get it back.

"Come," I said, going to the door of the tent. "The dead is alive."

The joy these words occasioned may be imagined. The Indians thought I had wrought a real miracle, and I did not contradict them. As One Feather led me back to the death tree he expressed his gratitude according to his standards by saying: "We will make you die in still greater agony than we had determined on. Never shall a man have suffered like you, and in the Happy Hunting Grounds you shall be the greatest of all the white warriors."

"Thanks!" I thought, but said aloud: "Had you followed Santer as I begged, you would have had him now, instead of which he seems to have escaped."

"We shall capture him; his trail will be very easy to find," said One Feather confidently.

Tangua had sent for Pida when he heard his medicine was lost, and after he had seen his father and wife on his return, he came to me.

"Old Shatterhand has awakened my squaw, whom I love, from death. I thank him," he said." but my soul is sick, and cannot be cured till I have my medicine again."

"Why didn't you heed my warning?"

"Old Shatterhand is always right. Had our warriors at least obeyed him today the thief would be here now."

"Pida will follow him?"

"Yes. Will you come with me?"

"Yes."

"Ugh! That is good, for then we shall surely catch him. I will cut you free, and give you your weapons."

"Wait. I can go only as a free man."

"Ugh! That is not possible."

"Then I will not go; Old Shatterhand is not a bloodhound."

He shook his head regretfully. "I would have taken you so gladly," he said. "I want to thank you for making my squaw alive, but if you will not go I cannot do so. You will wait here then till I come back."

He went away and when Dark Hair brought me my supper she said: "Old Shatterhand did wrong not to ride with Pida. It is honorable to die in torture without a groan, but Dark Hair thinks it is better to live honorably. Old Shatterhand might have smoked the pipe of peace with Pida on this ride."

"Don't be anxious about me; Old Shatterhand knows what he will do."

She looked down thoughtfully, glanced sideways at the guards, and made an impatient gesture with her hand. I understood; she wanted to speak of flight, but could not. As she raised her eyes again I said: "Old Shatterhand reads his young sister's thoughts. They shall be fulfilled."

"When?"

"Soon."

She was quick to understand, and said at once: "Old Shatterhand has not eaten enough. Will he have anything else? I will bring it to him."

She did not mean food, as I knew, and I said: "I thank my good sister; I have all I need. How is the chief's squaw?"

"The pain is leaving her head; the water helps it."

"She needs a nurse. Who is with her?"

"I."

"And will be all night?"

She understood. Her voice quivered as she replied: "I shall be there till morning."

"Till morning? Then we shall see each other again."

"Yes; we shall see each other again." she left me, and the double meaning of our words had escaped the guards.

Night fell, and the time was come. They had allowed me a blanket, and let me lie down, and as they untied me, and re-tied me in the new position, I slipped the little knife down my sleeve, and nearly severed the thongs. When all was quiet I pulled slowly, softly; the thongs broke; my hands were free. Then I cut the thongs around my ankles. The task was accomplished! The guards had fallen asleep, secure of me, because my wrists were too badly cut for me to break my bonds again. I gave each a quick blow to stupefy them, rose, and crept from tree to tree, from tent to tent till I reached Pida's.

"Dark Hair," I whispered.

"Old Shatterhand," she answered.

"Are my weapons here?"

"In the tent; my sister was so ill I had her taken to my father's tent."

Oh, the sharpness of a girl's wit! She waited for me till I came out with all my weapons. "How good you are to me, and how much I thank you," I whispered.

"Old Shatterhand is good to every one," she returned. "Will he come back perhaps?"

"It may be. If I do I will bring Pida with me as my friend and brother. Give me your hand that I may thank you."

She held it out, saying: "May your flight be successful. I must go; my sister will be anxious about me."

Before I could prevent her she had raised my hand to her lips, and slipped away. I stood still to listen to her footsteps; the kind, good girl! I crept away, found Swallow, saddled him, and led him out of the village till I thought it safe to mount. Then I threw myself in the saddle, and rode away like the wind. I was free!

CHAPTER XVIII

RETRIBUTION

THERE was not the slightest doubt in my mind that Santer would go straight to Rio Pecos, for in turning the leaves of Winnetou's letter I had seen that he had used Apache words in describing the hiding-place of the gold, which Santer could not understand, and for the explanation of which he would have to seek an Apache. He would run a risk in going, but such a man as Santer would risk anything for gold, and he had the leather case of the letter on which Winnetou's totem was cut, and which might obtain for his lying tongue the credence necessary to get the information he desired. So when I found myself a free man on the prairie once more, I rode through the darkness directly to Rio Pecos, although I could not see the trail of either Santer, or the Kiowas pursuing him. In the morning I came upon the trail of eleven horses; Pida and his ten braves who were on Santer's track, and were following him to Rio Pecos, although the Apaches were their deadly enemies, for an Indian must dare anything, and do-anything to recover his medicine charm if it is lost, since without it he is disgraced, and his life valueless. It was not long before I saw the little band of Kiowas ahead of me; they had encamped during the night to wait for daylight to see Santer's trail. I spurred my horse to overtake them, and when Pida recognized me he uttered a cry of surprise, and rode faster. I called to him: "Pida may wait. I will protect him against the Apaches."

Although he had shown fear, knowing that I was a chief of the Apaches, and had been his prisoner, yet he seemed to trust me, for he reined up, and called to his braves to stop. "Old Shatterhand! Old Shatterhand is free! Who freed you?"

"No one but myself," I answered.

"Ugh, Ugh! That was impossible."

"Not for me. I knew I should be free, and that was why I would not ride with you. You need not fear me; I am your friend, and will see that nothing happens to you among the Apaches."

"Ugh! Will you truly?"

"I give you my word."

"What Old Shatterhand says I believe."

"You may trust me. But I can only protect you if you are my brother. Dismount; we will smoke the pipe of peace together."

We dismounted, smoked the calumet, and then rode on to Rio Pecos. Nothing had changed. To the right was the grave where we had laid Winnetou's white teacher, Kleki-Petrah, with the cross we had placed over it still unharmed. To the left was the river where I had swam for my life; all was just the same in the pueblo where I had spent that peaceful winter, and had learned to know Winnetou and his people, but the three friends who had loved me were no longer there to welcome me. All the dwellers in the pueblo came with glad cries to make good this lack as far as they could do so.

"Old Shatterhand comes! Old Shatterhand! Hurry, braves, to receive him," they shouted, and a hundred hands stretched out to give me welcome, a sad welcome, for I had come without Winnetou, who would never see this beloved spot again. I found Sam Hawkins awaiting me there, much changed by the loss of his comrades, but delighted to see me.

"I have brought the Kiowas," I said at once, for I was anxious to make sure they were safe. "Pida is my friend; he has been kind to me while I was his prisoner. We have smoked the pipe of peace together, and I ask the Apaches to receive him for my sake."

"He shall be our guest as long as he wishes, but after he goes away he shall be our enemy again. How!" said Til-Lata, the new chief of the tribe.

"Good! That is understood."

"Now the Apaches will wish to hear of Winnetou, and how he died."

"We must wait for that, for Santer, the murderer of Intschu-Tschuna and Nscho-Tschi has escaped, and rode yesterday to Rio Pecos; we must capture him."

"The murderer! A pale-face was here yesterday and talked with Inta."

"It was he," I cried. "Take me to Inta."

Inta was one of the oldest men of the tribe. I did not know how Santer had happened to select him for his object, but he could not have made a better selection, for he had watched over the growth of Intschu-Tschuna and the young chief, and had loved them, and would have done anything for any one who had shown him Winnetou's totem.

The old man leaped for joy when he saw me, and began making me a long speech, which I cut short. "Leave that for another time," I said. "Was there a paleface here yesterday?"

"Yes!"

"And has he gone?"

"Yes!"

"What did he want?"

"He showed me Winnetou's totem on leather, and his medicine. He said Winnetou had sent him to learn the meaning of certain Apache words, which he did not want him to know till he had come here."

"What were they?"

"Deklil-to, the Dark Water, and Schisch-tu, the Black Lake, and I described to him these waters, which are in the depths of Nugget-tsil."

"Did you describe the way to get there?"

"Yes; it quickened my soul to talk of these places where I had been with Intschu-Tschuna and Winnetou, the chiefs of the Apaches, who have gone to the Happy Hunting Grounds. I shall soon see them again."

The old man was not to blame; he had only obeyed his chief's totem.

"Did the man eat here?"

"Yes, but not much; he had no time. He asked for cotton to make a fuse."

"Oh! Did he get it?"

"Yes."

"What was the fuse for?"

"He did not say. And we gave him a great deal of powder."

"To shoot?"

"No; to blow up something!"

"And have you the totem?"

"No; he took it, but he left Winnetou's medicine."

The old man brought out as he spoke Pida's medicine. The young Indian, who was standing beside me, uttered a cry of joy. "This medicine belongs to the young Kiowa chief. It was stolen from him; Winnetou never saw it in his life."

"Then I will return it to Pida," said the old man, "if Old Shatterhand is quite sure that is true. Was this man a thief?"

"Worse than a thief; he was the murderer of Intschu-Tschuna and Nscho-Tschi."

We left poor old Inta standing dumb with amazement and horror. Til-Lata spoke for the first time after we had left Inta's tent. "We will not wait; we will ride at once. Perhaps we can catch him before he reaches the Dark Water."

Pida was happy, for he had recovered his medicine, and had fully succeeded in the object of his ride. I wondered if we could say as much later. We parted with cordial friendship; Pida to return to the Salt Fork to his village, I to pursue the wretch who was still triumphing, and though I never again saw the young Kiowa, I remember him with liking and respect, and trust life has been kind to him, for he had the instincts of a noble man.

Til-Lata had brought with him only twelve braves, and Sam Hawkins had come with me.

It was evening when we reached Nugget Mountain. We ascended it by the first light of the dawn, passed through the ravine which I had rushed through on my way to rescue Winnetou on the day of the murder and came into the clearing where it had been committed. Here we left the Apaches, and only Til-Lata, Sam and I went on. We turned into a narrow fissure, just big enough for one person to squeeze through, walked some distance, and came out on the borders of a great lake, the presence of which one could not have suspected on the other side. It was fed by a hot spring, and its banks were dry and barren of all vegetation. Straight up from this rose a bleak peak, rocky and gloomy, surmounted by a crag. As we paused on coming on this scene, a shot rattled past me, and a voice from above cried: "Dog, you're free again! I thought I had only the Kiowas after me."

We looked up, and saw Santer above on the edge of the cliff.

"Do you want your Apache's letter, and to carry off the treasure?" he laughed. "You come too late. I have been there already, and the fuse is lit. I see you don't know the way up; why didn't you read the letter? I'll take the gold, and you can't stop me. This time I am victor."

What was to be done? It was true that we did not know the way, for the secret was known only to the chief of the tribe, and Til-Lata had not yet learned it. There was nothing for me to do but shoot, and I took my Henry rifle from my shoulder.

"Oh, you'll shoot, will you?" cried Santer. "Then I'll take a better position." he disappeared, and came out again higher up, and still higher, till he stood on the very apex of the crag. He held something white in his hand. "See here," he shouted..." here's your letter. I don't want it any more, for I know the directions by heart. I'll give it to the winds and the lake. You shall never have it." he tore the leaves into fine pieces, and threw them up in the air, and they slowly fluttered about, drifted down slowly, slowly into the lake. The precious letter! The last utterance of my dear Winnetou's faithful heart! I felt suffocated!

"You beast, listen to me a moment!" I cried.

"I'll listen with pleasure."

"Intschu-Tschuna greets you."

"Thanks!"

"And Nscho-Tschi greets you also."

"Thank you very much indeed."

"And in the name of Winnetou I send you this bullet; you need not thank me." I lifted my bear-killer; it was surer, and I must not fail. But what was this? Was my arm shaking? Was Santer rocking? Was the crag swaying?

I could not aim, and lowered the gun to look with both eyes. Lord of heaven! The crag swayed to and fro; there was a dull, heavy explosion, smoke arose, and, as if cast down by a giant hand, the crag, with Santer on it, toppled over, and crashed down, down, down into the boiling lake. We saw him throw up his arms, and shriek for help; the waters closed over him, and he lay under the mass of rock in the unfathomed depths of the Dark Water.

Sam gasped, his face livid with terror. "A judgment of heaven! He has died by his own villainy."

Til-Lata, who had been a little behind us, crept up to the edge of the lake, the bronze of his face pale, his knees trembling, and looked down into the waters which were seething and boiling, and said: "The wicked spirit has drawn him down into the boiling water, and will never give him back till the end of all things. He is accursed."

I could not speak; there were no words for such a scene. What an end for Santer! At the last moment I had been spared the necessity of shooting him; he had condemned himself, or rather he had drawn down the condemnation of the Most High, and had been his own executioner, for his hand had lit the fuse.

I was weak and faint; I closed my eyed and still saw the swaying crag, and heard Santer's scream. As soon as I was able, I crawled up and searched long and carefully for the scraps of Winnetou's letter. I could find but a few tiny pieces, with a disconnected word on each. That was all that was left me of Winnetou's long letter, but those scraps I have treasured carefully. We descended the mountain, found our horses, and mounted in silence. We were going back to Rio Pecos for a time, and then Sam and I would go East together, and my life among the Indians would be over.

The long rays of the setting sun rested on Nugget Mountain as we looked back at it from the prairie. Its wooded side was bathed in its golden splendor, the only gold that rested now in the secret recesses of its ravines. At last Intschu-Tschuna and Nscho-Tschi were avenged, and Winnetou's work was done. The Dark Water had buried in its boiling depths the murderer, and the gold for which he schemed, and sinned, and died. There was no longer a treasure of Nugget Mountain.

Printed in the United States
145140LV00010B/240/A